SEVEN

# WEEK 6:
# BETRAYAL

## Scott Wallens

PUFFIN BOOKS

All quoted materials in this work were created by the author.
Any resemblance to existing works is accidental.

Betrayal

Puffin Books
Published by the Penguin Group
Penguin Putnam Books for Young Readers,
345 Hudson Street, New York, New York 10014, U.S.A.
Penguin Books Ltd, 80 Strand, London WC2R 0RL, England
Penguin Books Australia Ltd, Ringwood, Victoria, Australia
Penguin Books Canada Ltd, 10 Alcorn Avenue, Toronto, Ontario, Canada M4V 3B2
Penguin Books (N.Z.) Ltd, 182-190 Wairau Road, Auckland 10, New Zealand

Penguin Books Ltd, Registered Offices: Harmondsworth, Middlesex, England

Published by Puffin Books,
a division of Penguin Putnam Books for Young Readers, 2002

1 3 5 7 9 10 8 6 4 2

Front cover photography copyright © 2001 Steve Belkowitz/FPG
Back cover photography copyright (top to bottom) Stewart Cohen/Stone,
David Roth/Stone, David Rinella, Steve Belkowitz/FPG, Karan Kapoor/Stone,
David Lees/FPG, Mary-Arthur Johnson/FPG

Produced by 17th Street Productions,
an Alloy, Inc. company
151 West 26th Street
New York, NY 10001

17th Street Productions and associated logos
are trademarks and/or registered trademarks of Alloy, Inc.

ISBN 0-14-230103-5

Printed in the United States of America

# CHAPTER ONE

**Dirt, sweat, grass** stains, blood, spit.

Reed Fraiser takes it all in as he looks around at his filthy, battered, battle-worn teammates. Each set of eyes is trained on him. Waiting. Salivating. Thirsty for his orders. His leadership. This is it. The last play. Do or die. The quarterfinal game and they're down by four. Ten seconds left on the clock. The team is tense. The team is pumped. The team needs him to win.

Reed is in the zone.

"All right, this is what we're going to do," Reed says, piercing each of them with his steady gaze. "We're going to run the three-out slant. Sha, you block that bastard like he's coming after your mother, you got me?"

Shaheem Dobi grunts and nods. The six-foot-two, 260-pound all-state linebacker he's been working on all day has been the team's worst nightmare, causing a fumble and sacking Reed twice. Reed can still taste the blood in his mouth, but it only riles him more.

"If he gets to me—"

"He won't," Shaheem says.

There is no trace of doubt in his voice. They're going to do this. They are. All Reed has to do is connect with one more receiver and his team will be in the semifinals.

Reed shifts his gaze to his tight end and wide receivers. "Just get open," he tells them, looking Jeremy Mandile squarely in the eye. "Get open and I'll do the rest. Ready? Team on three. One . . . two . . . three!"

"Team!" the squad shouts. They break from the huddle and walk to the line of scrimmage on the twenty-yard line. Twenty yards. That's all that stands between Reed and the promised land. That and two-thousand-plus pounds of hungry athletes out for his blood.

Reed licks his dirty fingertips, takes his place behind the center, looks up and down the line. It seems like the entire opposing team is ready to attack. They're coming on the blitz. That much is clear. But they won't get to him. They won't. He sees the play as clearly as if it has already happened. Three steps back, let it fly. He sees Jeremy catching the ball and stepping into the end zone. Hears the crowd erupt.

Reed takes a deep breath as a cold wind whips by, stinging his eyes. "Blue twenty-two! Blue twenty-two! Hike!"

The ball slaps into his hands. Heart pumping, Reed takes his three steps back, all the while looking . . . looking. . . . They're covered. All three of the damn receivers are covered tight. There is nowhere for him to throw.

2

Reed looks down at the offensive and defensive lines struggling with each other just feet away and everything goes silent. All he can see, hear, taste is the end zone. Then Shaheem throws his man aside. Tosses him like a side of beef. And there's a hole. A big, fat, wide-open hole. Reed looks at Shaheem, knows that Sha understands what he's about to do, and then takes off.

Cradling the ball, Reed slips through the hole and flies downfield, Shaheem running at his side. From the corner of his eye he sees a green shirt hurtling toward him.

"Right! Right!" Reed shouts, throwing one arm out toward the defender. Shaheem turns and with a smack takes the green shirt down. At that moment, two bodies hit the ground right in front of Reed and without thinking he leaps into the air, clearing them by two feet. Five yards . . . four . . . three . . .

Two more green shirts. Coming from each side. He's going to be crushed. Pulverized. He's going to be smashed in a green-shirt sandwich. Reed closes his eyes, takes to the air once again, and hurls himself over the goal line. He comes down on his right shoulder, clutching the ball to his chest as his helmet bounces against the frozen-solid ground. The two green shirts smash into each other and slam to the ground.

"Touchdown!" the announcer shouts fervently. "Frasier with the carry! Frasier with the carry!"

The crowd erupts into a cacophony of stunned, joyous shouts. When Reed opens his eyes, the ref is hovering over him, arms raised above his head, blowing his whistle like a madman.

Grinning, Reed pushes himself off the ground but doesn't even get to his knees before Shaheem grabs him around the waist and pulls him up, whipping him around in a circle like a little kid. Reed raises the ball above his head and shouts at the top of his lungs. The whole team surrounds him, screaming, thrusting their helmets into the air. Before he even knows how he got there, Reed is being carried off the field on his friends' shoulders as the cheerleaders and the home crowd rush toward him in a wave of blue and gold.

Reed scans the crowd, the grin on his face so wide it's causing more pain than any of the bruises from the game. Gemma Masters and Amy Santisi are screaming his name, and suddenly a blue-and-gold pom-pom flies up and hits him in the face. Reed laughs as he grabs it, but even as he does, he feels himself start to deflate. Because Karyn is not here. Karyn Aufiero never showed. The biggest game of his life, and the first game Karyn has ever missed. Cheerleading is like her religion. She'd rather die than miss a game. Yet she's not here.

Even though they're best friends, Reed and Karyn aren't exactly talking at the moment. But that doesn't make this hurt any less. Especially knowing why she's not here and where she is instead. In Boston, with his brother, T. J., her boyfriend—despite the fact that just a week ago, Karyn had kissed Reed. Yeah, he'd pushed her away. Yeah, he'd laced into her for kissing him and been furious at her for his

4

brother's sake. But deep down, there was a flicker of hope inside him that somehow that kiss meant there was a chance for the two of them. A chance that she might feel the same way he did. Then he heard she was going to Boston for the weekend to be with T. J., and it was all over. And now Karyn has missed this game, this play, this moment.

But then, Karyn isn't the only one who missed it. His mother isn't here, either. His mom, who never skipped a game when T. J. was the quarterback for the last three years. His father's not here, either, but that's understandable. His father has been dead for years.

Reed slips from Shaheem's shoulder and almost falls, but then a few pairs of hands reach up and help him down. Backslaps abound as the team jogs, still shouting their victory, toward the school, helmets raised in the air. Reed runs along with them, but the smile is faltering.

*Don't do it,* he thinks. *Don't start feeling sorry for yourself. Don't let them ruin it for you.*

"Reed!" Jeremy calls, jogging up next to him, grinning from ear to ear. "Coach Fedorchak says the scouts actually showed today."

"You're kidding," Reed says as he pushes his sweaty red hair off his forehead. He'd heard rumors that scouts would be at today's game, but he'd forgotten all about it once he was out there on the field, playing his heart out. "From where?"

"BC, Rutgers, Syracuse," Jeremy says. "Those guys must have *loved* that last play, man. You are golden."

Reed stops to catch his breath and puts his hands on his hips as his heart pounds against his rib cage. Karyn's image is wiped from his mind. Scouts. Actual scouts from big football schools. But they aren't here for him. They can't be. He's not a prospect. He may be good, but this is his first year as a starter. No one's going to take a chance on him.

"Dude! I have never seen a quarterback run like that!" Bobby Scorella shouts as he passes Reed and Jeremy. He turns to jog backward and laughs. "Coach already has those scouts up his butt for you!" he shouts.

*Scouts. For me.* Reed imagines what his brother would think of that. His mother. Even his father. Each and every one of them would go into shock. He's sure of it.

Reed's face burns bright red as he and Jeremy grin at each other. "See, man?" Jeremy says, slapping Reed's shoulder pad. "Golden."

• • •

Karyn Aufiero stands on the edge of the Falls High football field Saturday, feeling like she's watching everything that's happening through a crystal ball. Like she's watching her future. Or maybe her past. The overwhelming nostalgia that the scene in front of her is causing her to feel makes it seem more like her past. Like everything that has happened to her in the last twenty-four hours has somehow brought her beyond this school . . . this life . . . and now she's just looking back. Taking it all in.

She's not part of Reed's elation as he's carried off the

field. She's not one of the girls in tiny skirts, jumping up and down, hugging and screaming. She finds herself longing for the days when she was one of them, even though it was only last week. Is it possible, really possible, that just last week she was able to expend so much of her energy on locker decorating and pep rallies? It seems like ages ago. But as removed as she feels, the scene still makes her smile. She's never seen Reed look so happy.

She's also never been shut out of her best friend's happiness before, and it hurts like crazy. Hurts even more than everything that happened last night, even more than having to break T. J.'s heart this morning.

Taking a deep breath, Karyn pulls her cheerleading jacket tighter around her body and looks down at her high-heeled boots. Everything seems foggy. Driving for more than three hours on *less* than two hours of sleep had not been a good idea. But it wasn't as if she had a choice. She had to get out of there. She couldn't take all of T. J.'s questions or the sight of his sad, pleading eyes when she couldn't answer except to say that it was really over between them, right when they should have been closer than ever.

Karyn sighs and looks at the cheerleaders, who are packing up their stuff as the crowd slowly thins out. Coach Williams is making notes on her clipboard, undoubtedly listing everything the squad did wrong during the game. Karyn pushes her unwashed hair behind her ears and starts down the hill toward the sidelines.

"Karyn! Where have you been!" Gemma blurts out as Karyn slowly shuffles her way toward her friends.

Karyn shoots her a silencing look, crosses her arms over her chest, and walks over to Coach Williams, who's already eyeing her with disdain. The Falls High Cheerleading sweatshirt she wears is pulled taut over her sizable frame and she is, as always, wearing elaborate eye makeup worthy of a cheesy soap opera diva. Still, her comical appearance doesn't make her any less threatening. The woman, while a good coach, is pure evil.

"A little late, Aufiero?" she says, stooping to pick up her shoulder bag.

"I'm sorry, Coach," Karyn says, biting her bottom lip. "I had to go to Boston for a . . . family emergency. It was really last minute."

"Right. Like I haven't heard that one a thousand times," Williams says, not bothering to look at Karyn. "You could have at least called one of your teammates to let them know."

There's a moment of silence as the entire squad, which has ceased the normal postgame chatter to watch the throw down, looks at Karyn with wide eyes like she's about to be executed.

"She did!"

Karyn's heart thumps and all eyes turn to Cara Zellick. Little, annoying, eager-to-please Cara Zellick, who looks like a ten-year-old in her pleated skirt and ponytail and is turning purple as Coach Williams glares at her.

"She . . . uh . . . called me . . . this . . . morning," Cara fumbles out, her hands moving in jittery circles as if independent of her body. "I'm sorry I forgot to tell you."

*"Thank you!"* Karyn mouths over the coach's shoulder.

Coach Williams takes a deep breath through her nose. "So before the game when I asked the squad if anyone knew where Karyn was, you were . . . ?"

"Spacing?" Cara asks, raising her eyebrows. She giggles. "You know me, stupid Cara. Always . . . spacing."

There are a few titters from the rest of the girls and Coach Williams looks Karyn up and down. "Ten laps before practice on Monday. And don't be late." Then she turns on her heel and stalks toward the parking lot.

"Okay, so spill," Gemma Masters says the moment Coach is out of earshot.

"You really were in Boston, right?" Jeannie eyes Karyn suggestively as she slides up next to her. "I know a certain boyfriend who lives there."

Gemma's eyes brighten as the rest of the squad surrounds Karyn. "And we know Karyn wouldn't miss a game unless it was something important. . . ."

Karyn doesn't want to talk about this. With every fiber of her being, she dreads talking about this. She looks around the group of expectant faces, trying to find an ally, but even Amy Santisi, who normally runs interference for her whenever she's cornered, is looking at her with blatant curiosity. Karyn's alone on this one.

9

"You had sex!" Cara blurts out finally, jumping up and down with glee.

Karyn feels her spirit deflate as she looks down at the asphalt. "Thank you, Cara," she says sarcastically.

"Omigod! You did, didn't you!" Gemma squeals, grabbing at Karyn's arms even though they're still crossed tightly against her body. "Finally!"

"Details!" Jeannie says. "We want details. This is T. J. Frasier we're talking about."

Karyn's stomach turns violently. This *is* T. J. Frasier they're talking about. The guy she thought she loved. The guy whose heart she's broken. And the idea of talking about him like he's some kind of conquest makes her feel the need for a long, cleansing shower.

She looks up at her friends, hot tears filling her eyes. "We broke up, okay?" she blurts out, almost choking on the words. "We had sex and then we broke up. Need any other details?"

Eleven pairs of eyes just stare back at her in confused, stunned, sorry silence. Karyn turns and follows in Coach Williams's trail. She doesn't wait around long enough for them to find their words.

● ● ●

Jane Scott sits in the window seat in her bedroom, staring out at the leafless branches of a tree jutting across the bright blue sky. She sits there doing nothing. Nothing at all. Not worrying. Not studying. Not rehearsing. Not stressing. She's actually doing nothing.

Nothing except smiling.

A bird suddenly flies past the window, wings flapping frantically, and Jane blinks, startled out of her happy drifting. She leans back against the wall and realizes that the only thoughts she's had for the past half hour or so have been about Quinn. Quinn Saunders. For the millionth time, she feels the touch of his lips on hers and a warm, tingling rush passes through her entire body. She kissed Quinn Saunders last night. And he kissed her back—a lot.

She pushes her frizzy curls away from her face and crosses her arms over her chest, snuggling into her huge Falls High sweatshirt, letting the snapshot details wash over her yet again. Quinn's scruffy stubble against her cheek. The dark skin of her fingers touching his pale hands. The sound of his breath in her ear. Another chill rushes down her spine. Nothing has ever felt like this before. Jane is bobbing on a sea of giddiness.

Everything has changed. Just like that. Jane knows what it feels like to be consumed by something other than anxiety. Something other than stress, fear, and expectation. She's had her first real kiss. And Quinn—the very guy she's daydreamed about ever since she was old enough to realize that there were guys worth daydreaming about—wants to see her again. He's actually interested in her.

And suddenly anything is possible.

Jane pushes herself up and allows herself a nice, long stretch, letting out a contented groan as she reaches her arms into the air. But as her arms come down, her eyes fall on the monster stack of college catalogs and applications stacked on the floor next to her bookcase, and her spirits plummet. She may have been kissed, but it doesn't change the fact that she's going nowhere.

Narrowing her eyes, Jane walks across the room, picks up the pile, papers and slick brochures slipping all over the place, and tosses the whole lot into her closet. Pages bend and rip as they hit shoes and boots. The catalogs fall open, facedown, sideways. Jane doesn't care. She simply slams the door on them. She's done with the Ivies. Done with the conservatories. If there's one thing she remembers about last night—aside from all the kissing—it's how content Quinn had seemed. How calm. How at peace. How very unstressed. And why? Because he'd done the impossible. He'd gone against what everyone expected of him and taken a different path. And it had made him happy.

Jane takes a deep breath and plops down in front of her computer. Maybe it's time for her to take a different path, too. She clicks open her Internet server and starts searching for colleges. Big ones. Little ones. Liberal ones. Conservative ones. All far away from home. Far away from home and her parents and their picking and prodding and pressing and pulling.

There has to be more out there for her. For the first time in her life, Jane is sure of this fact. And she's going to find out what it is.

• • •

"So, we goin' somewhere to celebrate?" Shaheem asks, his slow grin taking over his face as he holds open the back door to the gym.

"Anywhere you want and it's on me," Reed answers, slapping Shaheem's shoulder pad.

"Yeah, they'd still be peeling Reed up off the field if it weren't for you," Jeremy tells Shaheem with a laugh.

"Jeremy?"

Jeremy Mandile freezes in his tracks at the sound of his mother's voice. A chill shoots from the back of his neck all the way down into his cleats. His mother, whom he hasn't talked to in days. She hadn't even called him on Thanksgiving, let alone asked him to come home for the holiday. And she shows up *now?* The woman has perfect timing. No better way to come down off a win than to talk to one of his parents.

It takes Jeremy about five seconds to turn around, and in that time his mind is filled with questions. What is she doing here? Has she come to apologize? To ask him to come home? Is his father with her?

By the time he sees her standing a few yards away, his pulse is pounding in his head and his last question has been answered. His father is nowhere in sight. Jeremy is not surprised, but he does feel ill. His fingers tighten around the face mask on his helmet as his mother clasps her hands together, releases them, and clasps them again, looking at him with a pleading expression he's never seen on her before.

"I'll catch up to you guys in a minute," he says over his

shoulder. Reed and Shaheem disappear into the gym instantly, obviously relieved to be spared the oncoming scene.

Jeremy takes a few steps toward his mother, doesn't get too close, then can't stand the longing he feels just looking at her and trains his gaze on the ground.

*Be a man,* a little voice in his mind yells. *You don't need your mommy. What's wrong with you?*

"You played a great game," his mother says, forcibly chipper. "That was an amazing catch in the third quarter."

"Thanks," Jeremy says, clearing his throat.

"So . . . I . . . I'm here to see if you'd like to come over for dinner one night this week," his mother says. He sees her open and close her hands again from the corner of his eye.

Jeremy glances up at her just as the wind pulls a chunk of red hair out of her low ponytail and starts whipping it around. "You mean, like a dinner guest?" he asks awkwardly.

"Jeremy, I really think we all need to talk," she says, lowering her voice even though there's almost no one around. "And now that everyone has had a chance to cool down . . ."

Everyone. Everyone meaning his father. But if his father has cooled down so much, why the hell isn't he here? The man never missed one of Jeremy's football games, caught as many basketball games as possible, and even took days off to come to track meets. Yet ever since Jeremy had told his parents the truth about himself a few weeks ago—ever since his father learned that Jeremy is gay—Jeremy

14

hasn't seen him at a single game. It's almost as if he's decided he doesn't have a son anymore.

Jeremy takes a deep breath and makes himself say it. "Where's Dad?"

His mother blinks. Flinches almost imperceptibly. "Dad couldn't make it today, honey," she says. "He . . . had to work. It's been crazy at the halfway house lately, and you know how your father is."

"Yeah," Jeremy says, his jaw clenching as he processes this obvious lie. "I know how my dad is."

His heart feels like it's breaking open in several places. His chest actually hurts.

"You can tell Dad that I'll come home when both of you are ready," he says, fighting to keep his voice even. "Until then, I'm fine where I am."

It takes all the energy left in Jeremy's already exhausted body to walk away from his mother, but he does. She's still calling his name when the gym door slams behind him.

# CHAPTER TWO

**"It's unbelievable," Jeremy** says on Sunday morning, leaning against the doorjamb between Reed's room and the hallway. His brown hair is sticking straight up in back and his left cheek is all dented and lined from his pillowcase. The T-shirt he slept in is on inside out and backward.

"What, your complete lack of grooming skills on the weekends?" Reed asks, looking up at Jeremy from his desk chair as he pulls the laces taut on his sneakers.

"Funny," Jeremy says with a smirk. Still, he pulls his arms inside his shirt and turns it around so that the tag, at least, is no longer sticking up toward his chin. "No. Every weekend, I get woken up by the smell of bacon and pancakes," he tells Reed. "Who ever heard of someone who doesn't cook anything but breakfast food, except for special occasions?"

Reed laughs as he stands up and grabs his well-worn Boston College baseball cap off one of the many hooks on the back of his door.

"What can I say? Mom has always been big on breakfast,"

Reed says. *Maybe because it's T. J.'s favorite meal.* "Besides, I've never seen you turn it down," he adds, trying to force his thoughts away from his brother and the instant mental link to his brother's girlfriend. . . .

"Hey, I'm just being polite," Jeremy jokes with an elaborate shrug as they head out the door for the stairs.

At that moment, Reed's phone rings and he turns to get it. "Go ahead," he says to Jeremy. "You don't want it to get cold."

Reed picks up the phone and says hello, wondering if he knows anyone who would actually be up at ten o'clock in the morning on a Sunday.

"Yes, is Reed Frasier available? This is Michael Cushman. I'm a scout for Boston College."

Reed sits down hard on his desk chair, stunned. He can't believe this. *A what? For who?*

"Yeah, I'm—this is Reed," he manages to get out.

"I saw you play yesterday, kid, and I gotta say, I like what I saw," the dynamic voice continues. "Now, I've already contacted the admissions office, so I know you applied to BC, but what I want to know now is if you've ever thought about *playing* for BC."

Reed's throat seems to have closed up completely. He attempts to clear it, stalling for time. Somewhere in his mind there's an answer to this question. There is. It's just hard to hear over the million voices screaming, *Oh my God! Oh my God! Oh my God!* inside his head.

"Reed? I do have the right number, don't I?"

"Yeah! I mean . . . yes! Yes, this is Reed Frasier," he says, sitting at attention. "But I think . . . I mean . . . you can't be serious."

There's a laugh. A big, rollicking, belly laugh that calls to mind random images of Santa Claus. "I sure am. You are the Reed Frasier who completed twenty-one of twenty-five passes yesterday and scrambled for a touchdown, right?"

"Uh . . . yeah, that's me," Reed says automatically. There has to be a mistake. There can't be a scout from Boston College interested in *him*. Boston College does not need quarterbacks. They have Maurice Howard, shoo-in for the Heisman, starting for them next year. And they have T. J. Frasier—*his* brother—as a backup. Why on earth would they be calling—

"Reed, I want to come down there and talk to you and your coach about a full scholarship and a potential starting position on the team next year."

Now it's Reed's turn to laugh. He leans back in his chair, thrusting his legs out in front of him. "Yeah, right. Very funny. Who is this? Chumsky?"

"This is no laughing matter," Cushman says. "Now, you know our starter, Maurice Howard? He got injured. We're talking career-ending injury. And we need someone to lead this team."

Reed swallows, grips the phone a little tighter. "I'm sorry, sir, but do you know my brother?"

18

"T. J.?" Cushman says loudly. "Of course I do. Fine young man."

Shifting in his chair, Reed pulls off his hat and chucks it onto his bed, suddenly sweating profusely. "Right, so what about him? Won't he be the starter?"

Cushman takes a deep breath and blows it out right into the phone, causing a rush of wind so loud Reed has to hold the receiver away from his ear. There's a moment of silence and the longer it lasts, the tighter Reed's stomach constricts.

"Look, kid, I know he's your brother and that this is a potentially awkward situation, so I'm just gonna give it to you straight," Cushman says. "We've been watching T. J., and he's good, but his heart's not 100 percent in it. He never would have made that play you made to win that game yesterday. I'm looking for heart. And you've got it."

Reed is frozen. Frozen in place, yet growing so warm he can barely stand to be in his own skin. He's using his free arm to grip himself around his torso, and his eyes are locked on a random spot in the middle of his carpet. All he sees is T. J.'s face. T. J.'s face when he got his scholarship from Boston College last year. T. J.'s face when he won the championship game. T. J.'s face when he first tried on his BC Eagles uniform for Reed and his mother.

T. J.'s face when he finds out his little brother is taking his place. Is in essence stealing his dream. T. J.'s face one of the many times he'd stood up to their father. Stopped him from—

Finally Reed feels able to speak. "I'm sorry, but I—"

"I can tell you're hesitant about this, Reed, and to be honest, I admire your integrity," Cushman interrupts, sounding like a true salesman. "But it can't hurt your brother if you just have a meeting with me. He doesn't have to know about it. And if you don't like what you hear, then fine, I'll walk away. But you shouldn't limit your options because you're worried about your big brother. I'm sure he'd never want you to do that."

*You don't know us,* Reed thinks. *You don't know how it works.*

"I'll have to call you back," Reed says. He hangs up the phone before Cushman can leave his number or even respond, then, shaking, quickly drops to the floor and detaches the phone cord from the jack so the scout can't call again.

He pulls himself back into his chair, feeling completely drained. He spins his chair around to face his bed and stares at the little eagle on his baseball cap, which landed perfectly, facing him. T. J. would die if he found out about that call. No. First he'd kill Reed, then he'd die.

Reed splays his legs out in front of him. For a split second, he allows himself to imagine running out onto the field at the Boston College stadium. He pictures himself in burgundy and gold. Sees himself completing a huge pass in front of thousands upon thousands of fans.

Slowly a smile spreads across Reed's face. There's a nagging edge of guilt trying to discolor his fantasy, but he doesn't let it. After all, it's not like he accepted the offer. He's done nothing wrong. And for once, he won't allow himself to feel guilty for his private thoughts. For once.

• • •

Meena Miller is having a hard time accepting the fact that she can actually relax. Whenever one of her parents moves somewhere in the house and she hears the creak of a floorboard or the squeak of a door, her heart seizes up in her chest. Then she has to take a deep breath and remind herself that he's gone.

Steven Clayton is actually gone. He's moved out. He is no longer a constant threat.

Meena shakes her head at herself and wiggles her way farther down into the couch so that she's almost lying flat, her head supported by a pillow. She lifts her history book a bit so she can see and tries to concentrate. She's still attempting to catch up after weeks of spacing, and once she reads over the first sentence of the chapter for the fifth time, she's finally able to continue.

*He's really not here,* Meena's mind sings like background music to her reading. *You're sitting in the living room studying and it's okay. He's gone!*

Without even realizing it, Meena starts to smile.

But when the doorbell rings a moment later, she slams her book shut and sits up straight to look out the front window, her pulse pounding in her ears. Thankfully, it isn't Steven's car in the driveway. It's a Mazda. A very familiar Mazda. Meena's already getting up when her mother answers the door.

"Holly! It's so nice to see you!" her mother says brightly, reaching out her slim arms for a hug.

Meena walks over to the doorway between the living room and the entryway. "Hey, Holly," she says. "What're you doing home?"

"Hi, Meen," Holly says, unwinding her pink-and-white scarf over her head and causing her straight brown hair to frizz out with static. "I was at my mom's for the weekend and I was just on my way back to Skidmore, so I figured I'd drop by."

"I'll make some hot chocolate while you girls talk," Meena's mother says, absolutely beaming. As her mom disappears into the kitchen, Meena realizes she's psyched to see one of Meena's old friends. It's not like anyone else has been dropping by recently, and with all the suspicions Meena's mother has about her, she must be relieved to see that Meena still *has* friends.

"So, how's school?" Holly asks as Meena leads the way back into the living room and sits down on the couch again, pulling her legs up close to her body.

"Fine," Meena says lightly, pushing her straight black hair behind her ears.

She doesn't really feel the need to tell Holly all the sordid details of how school *actually* is. That she doesn't talk to her friends, that she quit the swim team, and that she's in danger of failing all her classes. If she told Holly that, she'd have to explain why. And explaining why is not an option.

"O-*kay*," Holly says with a laugh, clearly surprised that Meena isn't elaborating. She shrugs out of her jacket and looks down at Meena's history book, scrunching her face up in sympathy. "God, I *hated* that class."

"Yeah," Meena says, crossing her arms over her chest and looking away.

It's not that she doesn't want to talk to Holly. She does. Holly's about the only friend she has left . . . not counting Peter Davis, who's pretty new in her life. But she's just not good at talking anymore. She's kept everything to herself for so long, she's not sure she's capable of holding the kind of conversation Holly's used to—light, fun, happy.

"You all right?" Holly asks, her blue eyes concerned.

"I think I'm just tired," Meena says. Her standard response these days. Tired or sick. "So . . . how are things with you?"

At this question, Holly's face completely lights up and Meena realizes that Holly has been waiting for her to ask. Meena smiles a small smile, relieved that Holly has something to occupy the conversation and that she won't have to try to talk about herself anymore.

"Well, I have big news," Holly says with a conspiratorial grin. "I am going to be spending a lot of time with an old crush of yours."

Meena immediately thinks of Justin Wigetaw, the

infamous crush she had for about three years. But that doesn't make any sense. Holly goes to Skidmore College and Justin's still in Meena's class at school. Why would they be seeing each other?

"Oh . . . who?" Meena asks when she realizes Holly is waiting for her to respond.

"Steven Clayton!" Holly announces giddily. "I'm going to be his research assistant!"

Meena feels like someone has just pulled the couch out from underneath her and she's fallen into a bottomless pit she'd never known was hidden in her living room.

*No, no, no, no, no!* Her mind screams it over and over again as she struggles to regain focus on Holly, who is now babbling about this dream job of hers. Meena's only catching snippets of Holly's words. The panic inside her is too much. It's like all her vital organs are climbing over each other in an effort to break free from her body.

"We'll be working late hours . . . private office . . . coffee breaks . . . wants me around at least ten hours a week . . . just him and me . . ."

Everything Holly says is giddy. Giddy and suggestive and blushy. Meena grasps the couch cushion at her side to keep from throwing up as her mind starts rushing ahead against her will. She sees Steven and Holly flirting. Holly smiling her half smile that boys love. Steven staring deep into her eyes. Then, in a rush, she sees them kissing. Steven pushing Holly down on a desk. Holly screaming. Holly struggling. Steven's pleading pout.

"You can't," Meena blurts out as the spinning room comes slamming back into painful focus.

Holly's face is the picture of confusion. "What do you mean?" she asks, picking up Meena's history book and absently flipping through it, not realizing they're actually discussing a matter of life or death here. "I can't what?"

"You can't work for him, Holly, you can't," Meena hears herself say. The words are coming out even though her mind is telling her mouth to shut the hell up. If she keeps talking, she's going to have to explain why. If she keeps talking, she's going to have to tell all.

"Meena, you're not making any sense," Holly says, closing the book in her lap and hugging it to her.

*I know*, Meena thinks. She leans back against the couch's armrest and presses her hands to her face. *Think. Think of something to tell her. Something that will make her run screaming in the other direction. Something not the truth.*

"Why can't I work for him?" Holly is silent for a moment and then Meena feels her shift in her seat. "Why? Because you still have a crush on him?" Holly laughs, dropping the heavy book on Meena's lap again. "Meena, you're so funny."

Suddenly Meena feels like she's going to explode. She tosses the heavy book on the floor, making a noise loud enough to startle both of them, but Meena doesn't care. She wants to shake Holly and tell her she's not trying to be funny. There's nothing funny going on here. Steven is dangerous. Steven will hurt her.

*"Meena, I thought we had something special. You made me believe . . ."* Steven's voice sounds in her head.

"God, Meena, what's wrong?" Holly asks as she glances from the book on the floor to Meena's burning face.

*Or maybe he won't hurt Holly,* Meena thinks, hoping for one single, rational thought. *Maybe he only wants me.*

Maybe Meena is the only one who brings out the monster in him.

"Here you go!" Meena's mother says happily.

Meena looks up to see her mother walking into the room with a tray of hot chocolate and cookies. She pauses uncertainly halfway across the room, the picture of the perfect hostess were it not for the trepidation in her eyes.

"Everything okay in here?" she asks.

"Yeah. We're fine," Holly says, dismissively, shooting one last questioning look at Meena. "Right?"

"Yeah. Fine," Meena says. She leans down to pick up her book as Holly focuses all her attention on Meena's mother.

It's clear that Holly simply thinks Meena is being silly. That she's just jealous of all the time Holly will get to spend with Steven. It's all too freakishly ironic. It wasn't so long ago that Meena felt that way—that she looked forward to seeing him. Just the thought makes her shudder. She watches, detached, as Holly and her mother dig into the cookies and gab about school, classes, credits, finals.

Her mother keeps looking at her hopefully, clearly wishing Meena would take part in the conversation—show some interest in Holly. In her future. In anything. But there is no way Meena can pay attention to the trite words and over-the-top enthusiasm spewing from her mother's mouth. All she can do is sit there and listen to the raging arguments in her head. Sit there and feel the pounding of her heart.

•••

"That's it! I can't take it anymore! I am getting her the bear!"

Peter Davis has just enough time to jerk his wheelchair out of the way so that Danny Chaiken can get by him on his way to the register in the packed-to-capacity Hallmark store in the mall. He watches Danny stalk up to the line, a big brown bear stuffed under his arm, and shift back and forth on his feet, trying to see how many people stand be-tween him and the register. He pulls out his wallet, looks inside the billfold, holds the bear up, looks at it, looks back at Peter, groans, and stalks, once again, to the rear of the store.

"I think that bear is going to have abandonment is-sues," Peter says as Danny puts the stuffed animal back on the shelf for the third time in fifteen minutes.

He didn't follow Danny to the register this time be-cause on the last two failed attempts to buy the bear he'd run over one lady's foot and crashed into a shelf filled with ceramic angels, causing mass destruction unlike any the manager of this particular store had ever seen. She, of course, hadn't made Peter pay for the damage because he's

27

in a wheelchair, but the woman has been eyeing him from the front of the store ever since.

Peter keeps shooting the scrawny little lady apologetic looks. He still isn't an expert at the intricacies of wheelchair navigation.

"Okay, we're outta here," Danny says, leading the way back through the store. "Excuse me! Excuse me, people, coming through!" Danny announces loudly, obviously expending some excess energy. Peter shakes his head as they emerge onto the brightly lit mall concourse. He's never seen anyone get so stressed about a gift before in his life.

"You made the right decision," Peter says seriously. "Cori Lerner doesn't seem like the stuffed animal type."

"I know, right?" Danny says, looking a bit relieved that Peter agrees with him. He runs a hand over his spiky hair and looks up and down the mall, searching for the next store to hit. "But she's not the Gap type, the Abercrombie type, the Brookstone type, or the CVS type, either," he adds, sounding desperate.

"Who, exactly, *is* the CVS type?" Peter jokes.

Danny narrows his eyes at him, his arms crossed over his chest. "I don't know—little old ladies addicted to hair dye?"

Peter laughs and Danny finally de-tenses long enough to crack a smile. He leans his head back and groans loudly, causing the guy working the wireless phone kiosk to eye them both warily. "Dude, what am I going to do? I have to get her *something*."

"Okay, what about jewelry?" Peter asks with a shrug. "All girls like jewelry."

"Since when are you such an expert?" Danny asks, raising one eyebrow.

Peter opens his mouth to speak, but he really doesn't have an answer. "Okay, so I haven't had a girlfriend since, like, the ninth grade, but trust me, okay? Women and jewelry. It's like the eleventh commandment."

"What? Thou shalt buy your woman jewels?" Danny asks.

"I've always kinda thought God was a chick," Peter deadpans.

"Fine. There's one of those accessory places down by Sears," Danny says, diving into the manic crowd of holiday shoppers. Peter struggles to follow. At school, everyone always gives him gigantic berth, which never makes him feel that great. But here at the mall today, it seems these people think it would be easier for *him* to get out of *their* way instead of the other way around. Don't they see he's a few feet wider than the rest of them?

Finally there's a gap and he's able to speed up a bit and catch up to Danny. "So . . . how are things with you and Cori, anyway?" he asks.

"Things are cool," Danny says. "I guess."

"You guess?" Peter asks.

"Yeah . . . I mean . . . she is just . . . so . . . cool, you know?" Danny says. It's clear from the thick excitement in his voice that there are a lot of feelings he can't express all

29

wrapped up in that *cool.* "I still don't know why the hell she'd want to be with me," Danny adds.

Before Peter can respond to this self-effacing comment, Danny stops in front of a store called Final Touch.

"This is it," Danny says, slipping into the little shop.

Peter starts to follow but stops at the front and decides to wait. The little store is crammed with small display cases and it doesn't look like it would be too easy to navigate. The last thing he needs is to send a hundred tiny earrings scattering across the linoleum floor.

"I'll wait here," Peter says as Danny makes his way to the shelves along the side wall.

"'Kay," Danny replies.

As he watches Danny carefully go through a display full of bracelets, Peter sits back and feels a smile stretch across his face. This has been a nice afternoon, hanging out with Danny at the mall. He'd been a bit surprised when Danny mentioned the idea at Faith Saunders's party Friday night and then even more surprised when Danny called him up this morning and he realized the guy was serious. He and Danny hadn't hung out in years. But a lot's changed for them both lately, and Peter's glad Danny invited him. Danny is a lot of fun, but he's also easy to talk to. He's blunt and honest, and that's not something Peter has found in very many people.

Suddenly Peter feels a warm sensation travel down his spine and spread across his back and into his arms. It fills his chest with a comfortable lightness and makes his heart swell. Peter just sits back and lets the warmth take over, enjoying its lulling sensation. A few weeks ago, when this first happened to him, it had left him confused and a little freaked. But now he's used to the random touches of comfort. He welcomes them. Each time the warmth comes, Peter feels a little bit better. A little bit more confident that someday everything will be okay.

Then, the warmth travels below his torso. Peter sits up straight as he feels it . . .yes . . . actually *feels* it run down his legs.

*This can't be happening,* Peter thinks, gripping his armrests tightly. He hasn't felt anything in his legs in weeks. Not pinpricks, not chills, not anything. His breath catches in his throat when the sensation leaves as quickly as it came. But he knows. He knows he felt it in his legs.

"Hey! What do you think of this?" Danny asks, breaking into Peter's racing thoughts. He 'd been so consumed, he hadn't even seen Danny return from the back of the store. Dangling from one of Danny's fingers is a circular Scorpio pendant hanging from a leather cord. Peter takes one look at Danny's psyched face and knows this is the right choice.

"That's it," he tells Danny. "I can definitely see Cori wearing that."

"Yes!" Danny cheers. He turns and steps up to the register where, luckily, there's no line and thus no time for Danny to think about it and change his mind again.

Peter turns his chair and looks out into the bustling mall, watching a couple of little kids as they play in front of a colorfully decorated Christmas tree. He thinks of the warmth and smiles, realizing that for the first time in his life, he's actually feeling . . . content.

It's the Christmas season. He's making new friends. Well, old friends who are becoming new friends, which is maybe even better. Everything is changing. It's as if finally, after all these years, he's actually being forgiven. The slate is finally being wiped clean and he's being given a second chance.

*I'm going to walk again,* Peter thinks, taking a deep breath. *I know I am.*

• • •

"So . . . do you think you're going to do it?" Reed asks as he pulls his legs up onto his living-room couch and leans back into the armrest on Sunday afternoon. "The dinner thing, I mean."

Jeremy glances over at him and his brown eyes actually look a bit scared. Even with all Jeremy has been through, Reed has never thought Jeremy would be *afraid* to go home. He just thought his friend was partially taking a stand and partially staying away because he was hurt. It's weird to see Jeremy scared to go home after all these years that Reed has spent envying his friend's perfect family.

"I don't know," Jeremy says, lifting one shoulder. "Emily would be happy. I feel so guilty every time she asks when I'm coming home."

*Guilty?* Reed thinks. *Why would Jeremy have to feel guilty? It's not like there's anyone at home he has to protect Emily from. It's not like she needs him to be there.*

"Yeah, but you've seen her just about every week since you moved out, right?" Reed reminds Jeremy, crooking his arm behind his head. "You didn't disappear off the face of the earth."

"I know, but it's gotta be weird for her, not having me around all the time like she used to. And I miss her a lot, too." Jeremy tilts his head and his face scrunches up quickly as he thinks it through. "I know she probably doesn't completely understand what's going on. I *really* don't see my parents explaining it to her. Even when we had that big fight, they made sure she didn't overhear anything."

"Yeah, I see what you mean," Reed says. He takes a deep breath and stares up at the ceiling, thinking for the millionth time that it seems like most of his friends are more mature than their parents. Parents are always messing up, being closed-minded, losing their tempers, playing favorites. . . . Where had adults gotten the reputation for being so mature?

"Why don't you just set something up with Emily again?" Reed suggests. "If you really don't want to have dinner with your parents yet."

Jeremy shakes his head. "If I do that now, I'll feel like I'm betraying my mom. You know, she invites me home and instead I hang out with Emily alone."

Reed's mind immediately flashes to T. J. *Betrayal . . .* That's pretty much all he's been thinking about all

33

afternoon—whether or not to go behind T. J.'s back and meet with Cushman. Whether he could even live with himself if he did. And whether he'd have the strength to turn Cushman down once he actually heard the offer. He's beaten himself up enough over that one kiss with Karyn— how's he supposed to deal knowing that he has the chance to steal away the most important thing in his brother's life?

The sound of a car engine fills the room and Reed looks at Jeremy, wondering who's pulling into the driveway. Jeremy's face is a blank, so Reed pulls himself up, walks to the window, and spots his brother just seconds before he bursts into the house.

"Mom? Reed? You guys are never going to believe this!" T. J. shouts from the foyer.

Reed's pulse is already pounding. T. J. sounds beyond psyched. Is it possible that the coaches changed their minds? Did they offer the starting position to T. J. after all? And if so, why is jealousy the only thing he seems to be feeling?

"Where's Mom?" T. J. says in lieu of a greeting as he rushes into the den.

Sure enough, T. J.'s blue eyes are gleaming and his cheeks are so rosy it looks like he ran the whole way home from Boston. But it's weird—there's something almost scary about that gleam in his eyes, something a little too intense. Reed pushes his hands into the pockets of his jeans to keep them from shaking and is about to answer his brother when he hears his mother's light steps running down the stairs. They all turn toward the doorway to the living room, and moments later she appears, obviously flustered.

"T. J.?" she says. Her glasses make her big blue eyes look even bigger, and she's still clutching the book she'd clearly been reading when he'd arrived. "What are you doing home on a Sunday afternoon? Is everything okay?"

*Karyn.* The thought flashes through Reed's head and his whole body stiffens. Karyn was with T. J. this weekend. Does that have something to do with T. J. showing up here out of the blue, looking about to burst?

"Guess what?" T. J. says, clapping his beefy hands together and looking from Reed to his mother to Jeremy like he's really expecting them to take a stab in the dark. For a brief second Reed has the crazy idea that T. J.'s going to announce that he and Karyn are getting married. He knows it's ludicrous. Karyn's a senior in high school. But what else would send his brother into such a frenzy? Well, just one thing—football. What if T. J. thinks—

"Maurice Howard, the idiot, ripped the crap out of his knee skiing!" T. J. blurts out.

Reed's stomach burns as he waits for the rest of the story to unfold.

"Who's Maurice Howard and why is his ripped-up knee cause for celebration?" Reed's mother says, looking a bit appalled by her son's reaction to such news.

"He's next year's starting quarterback, Mom!" T. J. says,

rolling his eyes but still grinning. "Or was. He's never going to play again. So I guess that means . . ."

"You're starting next year?" Reed's mother says, understanding finally lighting up her face.

"Looks that way!" T. J. says.

"Oh, honey!"

Reed watches in sickened disbelief as his mother reaches up to hug his brother, who is at least twice her size, laughing with glee. "That's right! I remember now!" she says when she pulls back. "Maurice Howard. He was that nice young man I met at the parent breakfast. Oh . . . what a shame. . . ."

*I guess that means . . . Looks that way . . .* Reed replays his brother's words in his mind, his fists clenching at his sides.

So no one's told him. No one's told T. J. that they're pursuing other options for the starting quarterback position. No one's informed him that they're not going to start him. They've just allowed him to walk around thinking that next year he'll be the new starting quarterback of a Big East team.

What kind of people would do that?

"Congratulations," Jeremy says, reaching out his hand to shake with T. J. When he pulls back, Reed is suddenly aware of a silence in the room and looks up to find everyone staring at him.

His heart skips a few beats and he makes himself smile. "Yeah, congratulations, man," he says, reaching over to hug his brother. His heart almost breaks when he feels how tightly

36

his brother hugs him. They pound each other on the back a couple of times before they both pull away awkwardly.

"Do you realize what this means, starting as a sopho-more?" T. J. says to Reed as they part. His cheeks are so red and his eyes are shining so happily, Reed is reminded of Christmas mornings when T. J. was still in footsie paja-mas. "This means I could get drafted, you realize that? I could play in the NFL!"

The burning sensation in Reed's stomach moves to his throat and he has to swallow hard to keep from being sick. "Yeah, man," Reed says. "I know. It's awesome."

As T. J. and his mother start to babble on about the possibilities, Reed sinks back onto the couch and brings his hands together in front of his mouth. As many times as he's thought about this situation today, T. J.'s cluelessness is a wrinkle he's never considered. He'd thought that at the very least, T. J.'s coaches would have the decency to let him know that they were on the hunt for a new starting quarterback. After all, they'd spent most of last year pursu-ing T. J., wooing him, telling him he'd be the future of Boston College football. Now it's like T. J. doesn't even matter to them. He doesn't even factor in. How could the people at BC do this to his brother? And how had he ever thought he could be a part of it?

# CHAPTER THREE

**"So, you want** to go throw the ball around with BC's new starting quarterback?" T. J. asks later, on Sunday evening. Reed winces as he watches his brother tossing his favorite football—the one that had been awarded to him as a keepsake after he'd won the state championship last year—back and forth from hand to hand as he grins at Reed and Jeremy.

"As much of an honor as that would be, I need to study," Jeremy jokes good-naturedly. "Some other time?"

"Yeah, man," T. J. says as Jeremy picks up his backpack and heads upstairs to his temporary bedroom. "Looks like it's just you and me, bro."

Reed clears his throat. "Yeah. I'm in," he says, even though he'd rather do pretty much anything other than be alone with T. J. right now. There's just too much—first everything with Karyn and now this. He's not sure he can handle listening to his brother gush on and on about his future prospects, all the while knowing it's possible he *has* no future prospects. At least not the ones he's got his heart set on.

Yet mixed in there somewhere, Reed can't help feeling like T. J. has the only thing that matters, anyway, starting position or not. T. J. has Karyn.

They head out to the sprawling backyard, covered with grass that has gone crunchy in the cold. The sun is just going down and Reed looks up, blowing a long breath out into the air and watching the fog it makes twist and turn and finally disappear.

*Maybe I should just tell him about Mr. Cushman's offer,* he thinks, glancing at his brother out of the corner of his eye. *He has a right to know.* Of course, doesn't T. J. also have a right to know that Reed kissed his girlfriend?

No, T. J. doesn't need to know any of it. Because Karyn's clearly made her choice, and Reed's made his—he's not going to take Cushman up on the offer to meet.

*Whatever T. J. says, you'll just listen,* Reed tells himself, rubbing his hands together as T. J. heads out farther into the yard. *You'll handle it. It'll be fine.*

"So," T. J. says, slapping the football once against his palm before letting it fly. "I slept with Karyn Friday night."

The ball whacks into Reed's hands so hard, it sends a jolt of pain up his arms. He holds his breath, waiting for it to pass, blinking against the cold as he tries to comprehend what his brother has just said.

Unbidden images of Karyn and T. J., clutching at each other under tangled sheets flood his brain and he squeezes

39

his eyes shut, struggling for breath while all the while trying to look like nothing's wrong.

*Okay, calm down. You knew this,* Reed tells himself. *You
knew she had condoms. You knew they were having sex.*

But no, wait. From what T. J. just said, it sounds like
this was the first time. Is that possible? But she had those
condoms weeks ago—why had they waited? Obviously it
wasn't about wanting it to be the right time because how
the hell could the weekend after Karyn kissed Reed possibly qualify as that?

Reed looks down at the football clutched between his
two hands. In all the confusion, one thing is clear—the
fact that nothing has ever hurt as much as his heart does
right now. His brother and Karyn. His brother and the girl
he loves. It isn't fair. It isn't fair that T. J. gets to touch her.
To know her every curve. To be with her completely. To
have her give herself to him . . .

He can't take this. He can't.

"You okay, Reed?" T. J. asks.

He looks up at his brother and his eyes narrow. God,
he hates T. J. He hates him so suddenly and so vehemently, he's shocked by the force of it. All he can think
about is hurting his brother. Making him feel the way T. J. has
just made Reed feel. Like the only thing he cares about,
the one thing he lives for, has been ripped away from him.
And ripped away from him by his own brother.

*Tell him,* a little voice in his mind taunts. *Tell him*

*you're going to be the starting quarterback at BC next year,
not him. Tell him about the phone call.*

"She also dumped me," T. J. blurts out. Then he laughs
and looks down at the ground. "But I'm sure you already
know all this. She tells you everything, right?"

"What?" Reed says, infusing that one syllable with a
wealth of anger and shock.

"So you didn't know," T. J. says, clearly surprised. Reed realizes that for a brief moment, T. J. is actually pleased to know
there is something between him and Karyn that she didn't tell
Reed about. That something between them is sacred. But Reed
is sure that T. J. definitely didn't want *this* to have to happen in
order for Karyn to keep her mouth shut. And he doesn't have
the heart to tell his brother that he and Karyn aren't talking.
That if they were, he definitely would have known.

*Wait a minute, we're not talking because we kissed,* Reed
thinks. He remembers the way Karyn looked at him right
before their lips touched. What she said afterward. *Didn't
you feel it, too?* Too. She didn't dump T. J. for Reed, did
she? But that doesn't make any sense, because why would
she sleep with him first?

This is too much. It's all too much to handle at once.

"Yeah," T. J. says, kicking up a patch of grass. "We had
sex and then she dumped me. The next morning." He
laughs derisively. "Pathetic, huh? It's been a weird weekend."

"I don't believe this," Reed says. His brother is now putting
on his standard "whatever" front, but he knows that T. J. loves

Karyn. He knows his brother is hurting. And one thing Reed has never been able to deal with is his big brother getting hurt. It's happened so many times, but Reed has never gotten used to it. It's why he can't fathom hurting T. J. himself.

How could Karyn do this to his brother? What kind of person does that to someone she's supposed to care about? Has sex with him, and then just dumps him the morning after? How callous is she?

*What if she did it for me? Then I'm to blame, too,* Reed thinks with a sharp pang. Then in the next second, he realizes that if she did it for him, that means she really does want to be with him. She really does want him—

Reed shakes his head. No. He won't let himself go there.

As quickly as his anger at T. J. had materialized, it refocuses on Karyn. He can't believe she could be so coldhearted. This is all her fault. His pain, T. J.'s pain, the uncomfortable, miserable silence that has fallen over this backyard game of catch.

It's all her fault.

Reed pulls back his arm and hurls the ball toward T. J., expending some of the pent-up emotion pulsing through his veins.

*"Weird weekend,"* he thinks. *Understatement of the century.*

• • •

They're all looking at her. Karyn can feel it. They have a million questions to ask her and they're not going to let it go.

It's Monday afternoon and her friends are talking about

last night's episode of *Alias*, but they're not into it. Their conversation keeps lagging between intermittent looks and whispers they think she doesn't notice. They want to talk about it. And when they want to talk about something, no matter what is standing in their way, it's only a matter of time before one of them caves.

"So, Karyn," Gemma says finally, in her practiced sympathetic tone. She lays her manicured hand flat on the table, the garnet ring her boyfriend gave her for her birthday glinting in the sunlight that streams through the window. "How's everything?"

*Code for, "I can't believe you finally had sex with T. J. Frasier! And why on earth did you guys break up?"*

"I don't want to talk about it, Gem," Karyn says, mushing her plastic spoon around in her yogurt.

"Don't you think you would feel better if you got it off your chest?" Jeannie asks, tossing her long dark hair behind her shoulders and leaning in to the table so she can see around Amy Santisi.

*You don't care about how I feel,* Karyn thinks.

"I mean, come *on!* Why do you think we ditched the guys?" Jeannie adds, succinctly proving Karyn's point.

Glancing across the room at their usual table, Karyn sees Reed sitting at the end, intently reading from a huge textbook while the rest of his friends attempt to crush oranges in their fists. Her whole body seems to ache with longing when she looks at him. Why had it never occurred

43

to her that dating his brother meant that when things went bad between her and T. J., she wouldn't have her best friend to talk to? Even if she and Reed *were* talking right now, even if they'd never kissed and she'd never realized how she really felt about him, she knows she wouldn't be comfortable discussing T. J. and the breakup with him.

But isn't it all connected, anyway? Didn't she end up sleeping with T. J. because Reed shot her down? It's not the whole truth. It's a lot more complicated than that. But at that very moment, it feels that simple.

"Was he bad at it or something?" Gemma asks gently, her green eyes full of mischief even if her voice is trying to sound soothing. "Is that why you broke up?"

"Gemma!" Amy exclaims, her mouth dropping open.

Karyn's face turns ten shades of red and she slides down a bit more in her chair. How is she supposed to know whether or not T. J. was *bad* at it? It's not like she has anything to compare it to. All she knows is it hurt, and it felt all wrong. And as she looks back at it, the whole situation—why she was doing it, how it was done, everything—just felt wrong.

"Come on, Karyn, you have to give us something," Jeannie says, as if Karyn is withholding information just to irritate them. "It's T. J. Frasier. You can't not tell us if it was good."

"You guys, just leave me alone, okay?" Karyn says, finally turning to glare at them. "Maybe it's none of your business."

Jeannie and Gemma exchange an offended look and

then refocus on their lunches. A tense silence falls over the table and Karyn feels an angry sob well up in her throat as her yogurt-mushing grows steadily more intense. What is wrong with these people? They're supposed to be her friends. Why do they always care more about getting dirt than they do about how she feels?

"That's it," Karyn says, her mortification finally getting the best of her. She can't take this anymore. She can't sit with people who'd rather give her the cold shoulder than give her a shoulder to cry on.

She stands up, scraping her chair back right into the person sitting behind her, and looks around the room for someone, *anyone,* to sit with. Her eyes fall on Peter Davis. In a split second she takes in the people he's sitting with— Danny Chaiken, Cori Lerner, and Jane Scott—registers the fact that she barely knows them, and decides that that could be exactly what she needs.

Karyn lifts her tray, dumps all the uneaten food into the trash can next to her table, and walks off, her friends calling after her in a chorus of condescending voices, letting her know they think she's being a baby.

*"Karyn,* come on. . . . Where're you *going . . . ?"*

But Karyn doesn't care. All she wants to do is talk to people who have better things to think about than what T. J. is like in bed. And she has a feeling that Peter, Jane, and Danny have plenty of other things on their minds.

• • •

"Wait, so you've just been ditching all your clubs?" Danny says, eyeing Jane as though she's just told him she's decided to cut a record and become the next Britney Spears.

"Like you've never ditched anything before," Jane shoots back, taking one of his french fries and munching on it.

"Of course I have," Danny says with a proud little head tilt. "I am Danny Chaiken, King of the Ditch. Master of Not-Getting-Caught. But we're talking about Jane Scott, God's gift to the teachers of Falls High. Do you even know what the word *ditch* means?"

Peter laughs and shakes his head, giving Jane an apologetic look. Jane doesn't mind, however. A couple of weeks ago, a comment like that would have gotten her all riled, but today it can't bother her. She knows that this is how people see her. That's who she's always been. But it's not how she sees herself. Not anymore. And she's starting to think that could be okay.

"Do you have a title like that for everyone in the class?" Jane shoots back.

"As a matter of fact, I do," Danny says, digging into his bag. "Wanna see?"

"Okay, you have *way* too much time on your hands," Jane says, holding out her hand.

She doesn't even know if Danny's telling the truth about having a list of all three hundred seniors somewhere in his bag, but it doesn't matter. Just *thinking* about having enough time to do something so fun and brainless as making up jokes about everyone she knows is so foreign a thought it makes her squirm. And that's why she's ready to change her life.

"Your loss," Danny says with a shrug, giving up the search. He and Cori exchange a smile.

"So . . . what's the deal?" Peter asks Jane, pulling himself a bit closer to the table. "You're trying to figure out what to quit and what not to quit?"

"Yeah. Well, you know I haven't been going to jazz band," Jane answers, looking at Danny. She leans forward and pushes her tray away with her elbows. "But I'm thinking that might be something I should keep."

"Good, because Missy Zambias is more than ready to stage a coup in the woodwind section and take over as first-chair sax," Danny says, munching on a handful of fries. "And you have to come back before Mr. Vega blows a gasket. Every time you're not there, he gets just a tiny bit redder."

Jane smirks when she thinks of the normally calm Mr. Vega losing his cool over her. And while Missy Zambias is a fine saxophone player, the band would not survive five minutes if Missy felt she had any sort of power.

"Well, I have to cut back a *little*," Jane says, pulling the collar of her wool turtleneck away from her throat. She tucks her chin inside it to keep it away. "I'm sick of running around like a psycho all the time."

"Yeah, I'm sick of it, too," Peter says, rubbing at his neck. "You're giving me whiplash."

Their laughter is interrupted when Karyn Aufiero drops into the chair next to Jane and lets out a loud sigh. "You guys mind?" she asks, glancing around at them. "If I spend one more minute with my friends, there could be a massacre."

Jane arches her eyebrows and looks at Danny, Cori, and Peter. She'd had no idea that Danny and Peter still hung out with Karyn, but she knows *she's* not the one the girl is here to talk to. She and Karyn haven't been friends in years, haven't had an overlapping class again after junior high, and haven't actually spoken since they hit high school.

"We don't mind," Peter says.

Jane simply shrugs. If they don't care, she doesn't care. She has nothing against Karyn. "So, what are you guys talking about?" Karyn asks, leaning her head on her hand. Jane can't help noticing there's almost a pleading quality to the question. Like, *Please let it be something interesting.* Well, she's come to the wrong table.

"We're discussing whether or not Jane will go to hell if she drops a few extracurriculars," Danny deadpans. "Your thoughts?"

Karyn looks at Jane curiously. "What are you thinking about dropping?" she asks.

"I don't know. That's the problem," Jane says, putting her hands in her lap and shrugging. "I just have too many clubs and I want to take it easy for the rest of senior year."

"Okay, well . . . which clubs are you in?" Cori asks. "Maybe we can help you narrow it down."

Jane takes a deep breath and looks up at the ceiling. Then she starts the list, ticking each one off on her fingers.

"Okay, we've got Academic Decathlon, the Web site, the jazz band, volunteer orchestra, math team, French club, Young Entrepreneurs . . . marching band, and . . . National Honors Society."

Karyn, Peter, Cori, and Danny look at one another in stunned silence.

"Oh! And the tennis team in the spring," Jane adds, lifting her hand. "But I can't quit that because I'm the captain."

Karyn tilts her head and widens her eyes, obviously overwhelmed just taking it all in. "Okay, well—"

"Oh! And my job," Jane adds.

They all gape at her.

"Sorry," she says sheepishly. Until she'd listed it all out loud and seen how the others reacted, she'd never really thought about how much she was really doing. What is she, insane?

"Done?" Cori asks.

Jane nods and takes a sip of her soda. "So, what do you guys think?"

"Drop it all!" Danny says loudly, swiping his hand at the air as if he's making a clean sweep. "Become a derelict. It'll be fun."

Karyn rolls her eyes. "While that's obviously a tempting option . . . ," she says with a laugh. "I think you should only keep the stuff that actually makes you happy. Like, think about each thing on the list and whatever makes you smile instead of stress, keep those."

"Oh, isn't that sweet?" Peter jokes, grinning at Karyn.

"Hey, I don't see you coming up with any better ideas," Jane says. She leans back in her chair and stares down at her tray, thinking through each activity. She's already quit Web site and jazz band, mainly just because those were the advisers she happened to run into last week when she was still coming back from meltdown mode. But it was never finalized with either Mr. Bonnebaker or Mr. Vega, and those are actually activities she gets some enjoyment out of. So maybe she could stick with those two. She thinks of her other activities, and when she pictures Ms. Motti and the Academic Decathlon team, she actually envisions herself pulling her hair out.

"Well, if we're going with the happiness plan, I definitely have to drop the AD team," she says with a laugh.

"Really?" Karyn says. "Why?"

Jane looks at Karyn out of the corner of her eye. "Because it gets *me* thinking massacre," she says flatly.

"Ah," Karyn answers with a grin. She sits back in her chair as well and reaches up to lift her long hair so that it falls freely over the back. "I don't know what the team is going to do without its brightest star, though," she says, playfully shaking her head.

Jane laughs with the others, but inside, she feels her stomach curl. Her father will freak if she quits AD. He's obsessed with her meets, her progress, her domination on the team. And he's not the only problem.

She imagines herself walking into Ms. Motti's room and telling the Hunlike woman that she wants to quit the team. Then, right in front of her eyes, Ms. Motti morphs into a scaly, green, saber-toothed closet monster and takes Jane's head off with one satisfied crunch.

*She's going to kill me,* Jane thinks, a more realistic vision of Ms. Motti vehemently lacing into her flashing across her mind. *And then Dad will kill me all over again.*

• • •

"You've got it, man! You've got it!" Peter Davis shouts, his voice sounding like it's coming from inside Reed's head as every one of Reed's veins struggles to burst free from his body.

"Come on! Come on!" Jeremy yells, hovering over the weight bench in the school's weight room, spotting Reed as he attempts the impossible.

Reed strains, using every ounce of strength he can summon to press against the bar. Each moment it feels like it's going to come crashing down and crush him, but each moment it gets a little bit farther away.

"Come on, man, do it! You've got it!"

Finally Reed lets out a barbaric, guttural growl and all the adrenaline rushes into his arms. He straightens his elbows and drops the bar into its cradle, gasping for air. Sweat pours down his temples and he almost swoons as he sits up, but Jeremy is clapping him on the back and Peter is laughing so hard they manage to bring Reed back to reality.

"You did it, man!" Jeremy says gleefully. "You just

benched three hundred and ten pounds! A personal record, I believe? Congratulations."

"Thanks," Reed wheezes out, wiping at his brow. He looks at Peter, who's just now gaining control of himself. "And you're laughing . . . why?"

"Man, I thought you were gonna pee on the floor!" Peter says. "I've never *seen* anyone get so purple."

"I'm glad my pain is so amusing to you," Reed says with a smirk. And even though he does mean it as a good-natured joke, he hears the venom in his own voice. Feels it in his blood. He's been like this all day—on edge, ready to snap. The unvented anger in his system is probably responsible for the dramatic feat of weight lifting he's just accomplished.

"Have some water," Peter says flatly, tossing Reed the bottle.

Reed knows Peter heard the bite in his comeback as well, but it's obvious he's going to let it slide.

He tilts back his head and squeezes the plastic bottle, filling his mouth with water. Then, just as he's about to move on to one of the Nautilus machines, he sees something out of the corner of his eye that makes his blood boil all over again. Karyn. Karyn is standing outside the little window that separates the weight room from the gym, talking to Amy Santisi. She's laughing and tossing her hair and Reed is suddenly filled with the desire to wipe the smile right off her face.

He can't believe what she did with T. J.

He blinks.

*No,* to *T. J. I can't believe what she did* to *T. J. And what* I *did to him.*

"I'll be right back," Reed says, dropping the water bottle on the floor with a thwack. He ignores Jeremy when he shouts after him, asking him where he's going. Reed has been avoiding Karyn all day, afraid of what he might say to her if he had the chance to give her a piece of his mind. Not wanting to make a scene. But now that he's seen her, he can't hold it in any longer. His so-called best friend deserves to know exactly how he feels about her.

"What the hell is your problem?" he says the moment he enters the gym.

Amy has disappeared, probably into the girls' locker room, and Karyn casts a wary look around the empty gym as she whirls to face him. The second she looks in his eyes, her skin pales. Reed doesn't blame her. He's sure he looks like a psycho, red faced, drenched in sweat, and angry as sin.

"What?" Karyn says, narrowing her eyes. She lifts her chin slightly and Reed feels like he's been punched in the gut. Is she actually going to be indignant about this?

"How could you do that to T. J.?" Reed shouts. "You sleep with him and then you just *dump* him?"

The indignation drops away from her face and she looks like she's about to throw up. Clearly she hadn't been counting on T. J. telling Reed everything.

"He . . . he *told* you about—"

"God, Karyn, he *loves* you!" Reed says, his face contorting

53

with disgust. "How could you do that? I mean, he wasn't just dating you to date you. He's in *love* with you!"

Suddenly the videotape starts up again in Reed's mind. The one showing T. J. and Karyn in bed, making love, kissing, touching, whispering to each other. Now *he* wants to throw up right here on the hardwood floor. Karyn clinging to T. J. . . . T. J. on top of her . . .

"I know," Karyn says shakily. "I . . . I didn't mean to—"

"To what?" Reed blurts out. "To be a colossal bitch?"

Karyn pulls back and her face goes flat. Her mouth drops open slightly and she eyes Reed as if he's the lowest form of scum. Reed, seething, feels the exact same way about her at that moment. In a million years he never would have thought Karyn could be so callous—so heartless.

*But so are you,* a little voice in his mind calls out. *You want her. You love her. You let her kiss you when she was your brother's girlfriend.*

"You are so not the person I thought you were," Reed says.

How can he love someone who would do these things? How can he *be* someone who would do these things?

Karyn takes a deep breath, her eyes shining. "I can't believe you're treating me like this," she says with tears in her voice. Reed feels a crack in his armor. He hates it when Karyn cries. "I can't believe you, of all people, could be so judgmental and just . . . *mean.*" She says the last word with an air of disgust, as if it's the lowest insult in the English language. "There are two sides to this story, Reed, but you don't even care. You're so busy riding around on your high horse, you can't even *bother* to care," she adds quietly, somehow managing not to burst into tears.

"I *do* care," Reed says. "I care about my brother."

He knows she'll understand what he's not saying. That he couldn't care less about her anymore. And he lets her believe it even though it's so very far from true.

"Fine," Karyn says. She waits for a moment. For him to take it back. For him to apologize. And he almost grabs at the chance, but he can't. It hurts just to look at her, and all he wants at that moment is for her to go. Finally she turns and walks off quickly, her head held high.

Reed puts his hands on his hips and looks down at his sneakers, trying to even out his breathing. Part of him is longing to go after her, but he makes himself ignore it. He can't comfort her. Not after what she's done to him. To his brother.

"What was *that*?" Peter says.

Startled, Reed turns to find Peter and Jeremy watching him from the door between the weight room and the gym, looking at him like he's just sprouted breasts.

"Forget it," Reed says, running his hand over his damp hair.

"It's gonna be kind of hard to forget all *that*," Jeremy says incredulously.

"Look, I know it's none of my business, but I just think you should know, Karyn hasn't had the best couple of weeks at home," Peter says, gripping the arms on his wheelchair. "I don't know what she did to T. J. or whatever, and I don't know if it excuses it, but you should just know that."

Reed feels a tiny stream of guilt seep through his mind. Last week, he *had* noticed that Karyn seemed a bit distracted and upset, but they weren't exactly on speaking terms at the time, and he'd figured that was part of it.

But maybe she'd been fighting with her mom again. Maybe she'd only gone up to see T. J.—only slept with him—for comfort.

A glimmer of hope appears in Reed's heart, but the moment it does, he's disgusted with himself, and he squelches it as quickly as it came. He can't think about this now. Things are too complex and convoluted as it is. He has enough to deal with without adding another layer to think about.

# CHAPTER FOUR

**Reed is running.** *He's running faster than he ever has in his life. He feels the wind whipping past his face, his hair being pushed back. He's scared. Petrified. Like he's running for his life.*

*He looks down and realizes he's clutching something. Something hard. It's a football. An old, battered football with the white stripes so worn down they're barely there. A football.*

I'm on a football field, *he realizes.* Then why am I so damn scared?

*He glances around as he runs, gasping for breath, sweat pouring down his face and neck. There are people on the sidelines. Faceless people. And they're all shouting something he can't understand. And even though he's moving as fast as he can, it seems he's barely moving past them. It takes what feels like minutes to pass each one by.*

What's wrong with me? Why am I going nowhere? *Reed wonders desperately. Whatever is chasing him is going to catch up. He can feel it. Feel it breathing its hot, putrid breath down his neck. Feel it gaining.*

He looks at his feet and sees that he's not wearing his football cleats, but a pair of impossibly tiny sneakers. Sneakers with Ernie and Bert smiling up from the sides. Reed remembers those sneakers, but he can't be wearing them. Not now. He had those sneakers when he was five.

"Reed! Reed, get back here!"

Reed's blood runs cold as the sudden sound of a deep, baritone voice fills his head.

"How dare you talk to me like that? How dare you walk away? I'm going to teach you respect!"

Faster, faster, faster Reed runs. He has to get away. He can't let it catch up. Can't let the voice take him.

But it's gaining. He can feel it. It's right there. It's on top of him. It's—

Suddenly Reed is tackled from behind. His face is mashed into the dirt. He's pinned down. The ball cuts into his stomach, causing him to lose his breath. Reed hears children's voices, feels a dozen tiny hands pulling at his clothes, his skin, trying to get under him. Trying to get the ball away.

Scared and confused, Reed rolls over, still holding the ball to his chest. His heart pounds when he recognizes the faces. Jeremy, Danny, Karyn, Jane, Meena, Peter. They're all tiny. Young. And they're all determined to get the ball. They scream as they rip and tear at him with their tiny fingers.

"Leave me alone!" Reed yells. "Get off me! Get off!"

Then there's a hand—a large hand—reaching between Karyn and Peter. Reaching out to Reed to help him. Reed *thrusts his arm out desperately, clinging to the ball with his other hand, and T. J. pulls him up. Reed's heart warms as he clasps hands with his brother. The screaming and the tearing and the groping stop. He's with T. J.*

*He's safe.*

*Then out of nowhere, the shouting starts up again, louder than ever. T. J.'s face goes slack with fear and Reed's stomach falls through the floor. He's never seen T. J. scared. T. J. is not supposed to get scared. And if T. J.'s scared—*

*A loud bang rings through the air and T. J. falls back. Reed stands there, helpless, watching his brother crumple to the ground, lifeless. And suddenly Karyn is there. She's seventeen now. And she's screaming. Screaming right in Reed's ear.*

*"He's dead! You killed him! It's your fault! You killed him! You killed him! You—"*

• • •

Reed wrenches his eyes open and gasps for air. He's covered in cold sweat. He pushes away from the pillow, lifting himself up onto his elbow as he struggles to control his breathing. What a dream. What an insane, petrifying dream.

In the hazy blue early morning light, Reed's eyes fall on his desk. On a framed picture on his desk. It's one of his favorite shots of him and his brother. Reed is about nine— T. J. ten. He can't see it all that well from where he sits, but he knows the picture like he knows his football playbook. The casual observer would never notice, but T. J.'s smiling face is marred by the fading remnants of a black eye—just the slightest tint of yellow at the top of his cheekbone and above his lid.

But both brothers are smiling. Arms around each other. Grinning for the camera. Keeping up appearances for the photographer. Keeping up appearances because it was all they knew how to do.

Taking a deep breath, Reed turns away from the picture and pulls his comforter up under his chin, facing the windows. He squeezes his eyes shut, hoping for sleep. Hoping for sleep without nightmares.

● ● ●

Meena rushes through the halls on Tuesday morning like a girl possessed, her eyes scanning the hallway for Peter. She notices a few people giving her freaked-out looks, but she doesn't waste an ounce of energy dwelling on it. She didn't sleep at all the night before. Didn't eat a thing this morning. Hasn't been able to think about anything except Holly.

Clueless, innocent Holly.

All the little hairs on Meena's skin stand up when she thinks about her friend. She never knew it was possible to be this scared for someone else.

Rounding the corner into the hallway where Peter's locker is, Meena almost plows over two unsuspecting sophomores. They part just in time and she slips between them, whacking one of them with her shoulder.

"Excuse *me!*" the blonder of the two fake blonds says sarcastically.

Peter looks up at the sound of the loud comment, and Meena's gaze meets his. Peter's face registers alarm the moment he sees her.

"What is it?" he asks, shakily closing the notebook in his lap.

"Can we go somewhere?" Meena asks quietly, looking down at him through the blanket of her hair.

Peter glances quickly from left to right, then spins one wheel to turn his chair around and slaps his locker closed with a bang. "C'mere," he says, tilting his head. "They don't have a homeroom in here."

Meena follows Peter into an empty English classroom and closes the door behind them, leaving the lights off. She doesn't want to call any kind of attention to their little conversation.

"What's going on?" Peter asks, his fingers curling around the ends of his armrests.

"Do you remember Holly Finneran?" Meena asks, pushing her hair behind her ears. She stuffs her hands into the back pockets of her jeans, then pulls them out again to fiddle with the cord hanging from the hood of her sweatshirt. She hasn't been able to stop fidgeting all morning.

Peter blinks. Ponders. "Not really," he says slowly. "Why?"

"Well, she's a really good friend of mine and she goes to the school where Steven Clayton teaches, and she came over to my house yesterday afternoon to tell me she's going to be his research assistant," Meena says all in one breath, wrapping her arms around herself.

"That's not good," Peter says.

"It's not good on so many levels," Meena says, walking over to the window and back again. Over to the window and back again. "She's excited about it. Like, little-girl-with-a-crush excited. She was talking about private offices and late night coffee breaks. . . ."

Meena trails off, the images crowding her brain again. Holly and Steven. Holly and Steven. Holly and—

"What am I supposed to do?" Meena says, her voice coming out as a whine. She drops down behind one of the desks and puts her head in her hands. "I mean, they're going to be alone together all the time. Late at night. Alone! And Holly doesn't know anything about him. She just thinks he's some . . . *hottie.*"

"Hottie?" Peter asks, raising his eyebrows.

Meena's skin burns and she looks down at the fake wood desk. The little etchings of boredom along the out-side rim—*Jay-Z rulz. WWJD?* "We always thought he was so cool . . . growing up. We both . . ."

She can't finish the sentence. She can't admit out loud that she'd had a silly, childish crush on the man. That she had a crush on a person who turned out to be a monster.

"Okay . . . okay," Peter says in a soothing voice. "What are you going to do?"

A sob wells up in Meena's throat and she swallows it

back, standing up again and turning away from him. Her voice sounds wet and tearful when she speaks again.

"I don't know!" she says, throwing her hands up and letting them slap back down against her thighs. She starts to pace, pushing her hands into her hair and holding it back from her face as she tries to make sense of her warring thoughts.

"I'd kill myself if anything happened to her," she says, glaring down at the floor.

"So you have to warn her," Peter says.

His words make Meena freeze in her tracks even though she's been thinking the same thing all night.

"I can't," she says, one tear spilling over. "I can't tell anyone what happened."

Just the thought makes her so scared, she wants to curl up in a little ball and hide under the big metal desk at the front of the classroom. How could she? How could she ever say the words?

*He raped me. I thought he liked me and I flirted with him and he raped me.* Thinking the words makes her throat close up.

"You told *me* something happened," Peter says quietly. Tentatively. He looks at her, then glances away, then looks back again, this time holding her gaze steadily. Holding her gaze with his beautiful, clear, confident green eyes.

Meena gazes back, thinking how ignorant Peter actually is about the situation. She knows he means well, but he doesn't know anything. She never spelled it out for him. Never actually came out and said it. He doesn't know what really happened. Doesn't know how it's destroyed her. Doesn't know how it's made her afraid to sleep. Doesn't know how much Steven actually took from her or how violently he did it.

"That's different," she says finally, pulling her eyes away from his to find the floor once again. "If I tell Holly, I'll have to tell her . . . everything."

The word *everything* hangs in the air like a guillotine blade about to drop. Peter takes a deep breath. It's clear he's thinking through every word before he says it.

"You're right," he says. "And I know it will be hard. It's different because Holly *has* to know. She's putting herself in a dangerous situation, and you're the only one who can protect her."

Meena's shoulders curl forward under the weight of his words and she starts to cry silently. Because she knows he's right. She knows she has to help Holly. But why? Why is this happening to her? She'd thought it had ended when Steven and his family moved out. She'd thought she'd be able to somehow move on. Maybe even one day forget. But now . . . now it's all rushing back again, and she is going to have to deal with it. Holly has given her no choice.

*No, Steven has given me no choice.*

Peter reaches out his hand toward hers, which is now hanging limply at her side. As she sees his fingers approach her own, she flinches and for a split second thinks of pulling away. But she doesn't. For some reason, she doesn't move. She lets Peter touch her.

The warmth of his skin seems to penetrate her as his fingers wrap around hers. A rushing, tingling sensation runs up her arm and over her shoulders, and Meena draws in a long, shuddering, relieved breath.

No one has touched her in weeks. She hasn't let it happen. But Peter's touch is comforting. And Meena suddenly finds herself wishing she could hold his hand all day long.

"I can't tell you what to do. I don't even know what *I* would do," Peter says, his voice low and filled with compassion. It sends another tingling wave over her. "But I know you're going to figure it out and do the right thing." He squeezes her hand and holds her with his serious, rock-solid gaze. "I know you are."

Meena, to her own surprise, squeezes back. She only wishes she were so sure.

• • •

"Frasier! In my office. *Now!*"

Reed's heart falls as he looks up at Coach Fedorchak, who's standing, barrel chest thrust out, in the doorway between the locker room and his office. The man looks like a pit bull salivating over a steak, his eyes bulging and the large vein in his neck throbbing. Reed watches his Adam's apple move up and down as he swallows.

"What did you do, man?" Shaheem Dobi asks, a look of trepidation in his dark eyes as Coach disappears into his office and starts slamming stuff around on his desk. Fedorchak is pretty much the only person on the planet capable of making Sha look nervous.

"I don't know," Reed says. He pulls his T-shirt on over his head and pushes his hand through his damp hair, watching the open office door. He's still a bit wet from the shower, and the shirt sticks to him as the dampness goes up a notch out of nervousness. He mentally reviews the last two practices, wondering what he could have possibly done to incite the wrath of Coach.

"Well, good luck," Shaheem says, grabbing his backpack and heading for the hallway. He pops his signature toothpick into his mouth and rolls it around. "If he kills you, can I have your car?" he adds with a grin.

"Ha ha," Reed says, narrowing his eyes.

He takes a deep breath and slips his arms into the sleeves of his flannel, letting it hang open to keep himself cool. Then he picks up his own bag and walks over to Fedorchak's office, pulling his baseball cap down tightly over his forehead. *Whatever he says, just yes him to death,* he tells himself. *There's never any use in arguing with the guy.* He clears his throat, straightens his back and rounds his shoulders, then crosses the threshold like he's walking the plank.

"What's up, Coach?" Reed asks, shoving one hand into the front pocket of his jeans and clutching his backpack strap with the other.

Coach Fedorchak sits down and leans back in his rickety wooden chair, causing a loud, nerve-splitting creak. He folds his hands over his stomach, resting them on his gray sweat-shirt, then, blowing out a sigh, he finally looks at Reed.

"Sit down, son," he says, flicking his brown eyes toward the chair across from his desk.

Reed's in the seat in less than a second. He still has no idea why he's here, but there's no reason not to obey direct orders. He rests his bag in his lap and sits on the edge of the chair, his feet firmly on the floor, like he's ready to run if he needs to.

"I got an interesting phone call today," Coach says, nodding absently as if he's going over the telephone conversation in his mind. "It was from a scout at BC."

Reed blinks and grips the coarse fabric of his backpack in his hand as he absorbs this information. The BC people called his coach? What are they doing, stalking him? Didn't they get the picture when he hadn't called them back?

*They must really want me,* Reed realizes, his heart both warming and twisting painfully.

"Why didn't you tell me they called you, Reed?" Coach asks, leaning forward in his seat and resting his elbows on top of his cluttered desk. "This is a huge, *huge* deal." With each word he thrusts the tip of his calloused index finger against the desktop.

Reed pulls his gaze away from Coach's hands and meets his eyes. What he sees there surprises him so thoroughly, little butterflies take flight in his stomach. Coach Fedorchak looks excited. He looks . . . happy.

How is that possible? T. J. was one of Fedorchak's

favorite players. Ever. In the history of Falls High football, T. J. was Fedorchak's number-one golden boy.

Or so Reed had thought.

"An offer from Boston College is not something that should be taken lightly," Coach says, his face growing red with excitement as he rises from his chair. "Do you know how many pro players have gone there? How many bowls they've won? And they're on the rise, Reed. You could take them back to the top. You! Just imagine it. . . ."

As Coach continues to babble on about the possibilities, Reed feels himself squirming in his seat, unable to get comfortable. Unable to get comfortable in his own skin. Each word is like a pinch that makes him tense up a little bit more.

*You can't do this,* a little voice in his mind tells him, trying to block out Fedorchak's excited voice. *You can't do this to T. J. Not after everything he's done for you. Everything he's put himself through to spare you.*

"Starting as a freshman . . . Dream come true . . . You can't even *think* of turning this down. . . ."

This is just like the last time. That one time last year when Fedorchak had called Reed into his office and made him an offer. An offer he thought Reed couldn't refuse. But Reed hadn't been able to accept the fact that he might be as good as his brother. That he might be able to take T. J.'s place. Now he starts to wonder. Can he do it? Is it possible? Could he really be as good a player as the legendary T. J. Frasier?

*No,* Reed tells himself, clenching his jaw. *You aren't as good as T. J. You can't be. You'll never be as good as T. J.* He *deserves the spot at BC.* He *deserves to start.*

Reed watches Coach Fedorchak pace the room, gazing at framed photos and certificates and newspaper articles as he always does when he's on a roll. As if remembering his past glories feeds the fire of his lectures. And the longer Reed watches him, the more disgusted he becomes. How can Coach talk to him like this? How can he encourage him to do it? To take the spot away from T. J.? To take away everything T. J. has ever worked for?

Coach and T. J. had been like father and son.

*How could he? What is this guy's problem?*

Reed's fingers grip tighter onto his backpack as he tells himself to chill. All he has to do is let Coach Fedorchak finish, politely tell him that he's not interested in BC, and get the hell out of here. All he has to do is stay calm. . . .

"This is it, Reed. This is your chance. All you have to do is—"

*Screw over my brother.*

And then Reed can't take it anymore. He pushes himself out of his chair and looks Coach Fedorchak squarely in the eye.

"You haven't mentioned T. J.," Reed says, his jaw clenching and unclenching as he glares at the coach.

Fedorchak blinks and takes a step back. Reed is sure no one has ever interrupted the coach before, let alone challenged him.

"Well, your brother is a fine player," Fedorchak tells

69

him, a bit flustered. "But if BC wants you, they want you. I'd think you'd be more excited, Reed. After only one year of starting and you—"

"I'm not interested in Boston College, Coach," Reed says, slinging his bag over his shoulder. His coach's eyes widen in disbelief and his jaw hangs open just slightly. "And if they call you again, I'd appreciate you telling them that," Reed adds.

He brushes past the coach and out the door before the man can say another word to confuse him. The sound track of what he's just said is playing over and over again in Reed's mind already.

*Your chance . . . your dream . . . an honor . . . how many professional players . . . how many bowls . . .*

Reed wants it so badly, he can taste it. He's actually salivating. But he can't. He can't take away the thing that matters most to his brother—especially when T. J. has just lost the only other thing he cares about—Karyn. Not after everything they've been through. Not after everything T. J. has done for him. Reed can do anything, be anyone, go anywhere. He's got brains. He's got the ability to be whatever he wants.

But all T. J. has is football. It's his brother's only hope for a future. And Reed is not going to get in his way. After everything they've been through, Reed owes his brother that much.

The moment he's through the door, Reed finds himself

face-to-face with Jeremy, whose face pales with guilt. They just stand there for a moment and Reed knows Jeremy was listening. That he's heard everything. Suddenly the guilt falls away from Jeremy's features and is replaced with an open, honest challenge. He wants to know why Reed didn't tell him about this. He wants to know what Reed is thinking, blowing his chance.

But Reed's not about to answer his questions. He's not about to let Jeremy put his two cents in. He slides by his friend and out the door, jogging down the hall toward the main exit. The last thing he needs is another voice in his head. Thanks to Coach, he's conflicted enough as it is.

• • •

Jeremy leans back on the hood of his car Tuesday afternoon and checks his watch for the fifteenth time in the last ten minutes. He can't seem to stop himself from looking at it.

*What am I doing here?* he asks himself, rubbing his dry hands together to combat the cold. The rest of the ballet school parents are sitting in their idling cars, warm and comfortable, waiting for their daughters and sons to emerge. Not Jeremy. Jeremy wants to be sure that he can get to Emily the second she walks out. He figures he'll talk to her for a minute, see how she is, and then bolt before his mother or father arrives to pick her up. It's their day for carpool.

*I can't believe this is my life,* Jeremy thinks as the doors to the little school finally fly open, producing a stream of tiny, tutued girls and a couple of untutued boys. *Stealing time with my sister. Afraid to see my parents. This is pathetic.*

He's about to start feeling seriously sorry for himself when he sees Emily running toward him, her face one big, freckled smile. He feels like she's tugging his heart right out of his body. And when she shouts his name and reaches up to hug him, he's so happy, he forgets all about his watch.

"Man, it's good to see you," Jeremy says, hugging her so hard she could very well break.

"What are you doing here?" she asks excitedly as she pulls back. "Are you picking me up? Are you coming home?"

Jeremy feels a pang of guilt at her innocent questions and her breathlessness, but he manages to keep the smile plastered to his face. "Not today," he says. "But let's not talk about that," he adds quickly when her face starts to fall. "What's going on with you?"

She sucks in an audible breath and starts to babble, fast and furious like a bee that's just been set free from a glass jar. "Miss Lindstrom had me show everyone how to pirouette today in class," she says. "And Olive Howard and Terra Blattberg were *so* jealous. And I got an A on my spelling test and a B in math, which means I beat Mark Gillus on my report card and he's *so* mad, and he says he's never going to talk to me again, but I don't care because I *hate* him, anyway. And I—"

"Okay! Okay! Slow down," Jeremy says with a laugh. "Breathe for a second."

"Well, I have a lot to *tell* you," Emily says, putting her

72

hands on her hips. "It's not like I ever *see* you," she says, rolling her eyes. She looks up at him sadly and Jeremy feels that little tug at his heart all over again.

"When *are* you coming home?" she asks.

Jeremy sighs, trying not to look as upset and guilty as he feels. "I'm not really sure," he says, not wanting to lie to her.

The already sad look on her face deepens and Jeremy picks her up in his arms and hugs her, even though she's probably too big at this point to be picked up. But she doesn't protest, so he doesn't stop. Then he notices something over her shoulder and freezes. His mother is there, standing outside her own car, and she's watching them with a look of hope on her face that breaks Jeremy's heart.

He puts Emily down, shaking. Frustration surges through him. Forget his dad. He can't handle making his mother and sister this unhappy. Not when there's something he can do about it. So what if his father didn't come to his game?

Jeremy can be the bigger man here.

He reaches out and holds Emily's hand, and together they walk across the parking lot to his mother.

"Hey, Mom," he says.

"Hi, Jeremy," she returns. She clutches the top of her open car door, watching him. Waiting for him to make the first move.

He glances down at Emily and squeezes her hand. "So . . . when did you want to have that family dinner?"

# CHAPTER FiVE

**Don't ask me** *about it. Just don't.*

Reed places the forks and knives down on the table Tuesday evening, making sure each one is evenly spaced away from its plate and lined up perfectly straight, all to avoid having to look at Jeremy. He knows that if he just glances at him, his friend will have that questioning, accusing, we-have-to-talk look in his eye, and he's not about to deal with that. Not now. In fact, he'd much prefer it if he didn't have to deal with it ever.

"Done," Reed says, wiping his moist palms on the legs of his jeans. He's already started turning toward the door to retreat. "Call me when dinner's ready. I'll be—"

"Wait. You need one more place," his mother says as she unpacks the upscale takeout she'd ordered and places the salmon in the oven to warm up. "T. J. called. He's coming home for the night. He should be here any minute."

All the blood rushes out of Reed's face and he finds himself reaching out one hand to grip the top of the chair next to him. Why is T. J. coming home *again?* Have his coaches finally told him they called Reed and offered him a spot on the team? Is he coming home to kick Reed's ass? Or is it Karyn—is he coming because Karyn said she wants to get back together? Reed actually doesn't know which would be worse. But his gut tells him this isn't about Karyn.

*Man, why couldn't he have gone to UCLA or something?* The three-hour drive from Boston is like nothing to his brother in his loaded SUV. If he'd gone to a different school, he wouldn't have been *able* to come home and kick Reed's ass.

"Doesn't he have classes?" Reed hears himself blurt out. His voice sounds oddly strained.

His mother straightens up and closes the oven, then turns slowly to level Reed with a glare that tells him it's not his place to question his brother's comings and goings. Then she shakes her hair back from her head, even though there's never a single strand out of place, and returns to one of the aluminum dishes on the counter.

"Finals are coming up, Reed," she says, digging into the rice and mixing it around. "T. J.'s regular classes are over, so he has more free time." She sighs, pushes the dish away, and pops open another container. "You know, I'd think you'd be happy T. J. is home so much. We didn't think we'd be seeing him at all when he decided to go to BC."

The blood rushes back to Reed's face full force and he finally glances at Jeremy, who's silently setting a place for T. J. at the head of the table. Reed clenches and unclenches

75

his jaw, trying to figure out what he's going to say to T. J. when he confronts him.

*You haven't done anything wrong,* a little voice in Reed's head reminds him. *You won't even talk to the guys at BC. You're blameless here. Blameless.*

Reed closes his eyes, pushes the brim of his cap up with his knuckle, and rubs at his forehead. He stopped that kiss with Karyn, even as every part of his being screamed for him to never let go of her. And it's not like he had any control over the fact that *she* kissed *him* or like he asked the Boston College people to recruit him. *Blameless,* he thinks again. But if he's so blameless, then why does he feel so damn guilty?

"Hi, honey, I'm home!" T. J.'s voice suddenly bellows from the foyer.

Reed's breath catches in fear for one, irrational split second, but then the boisterous quality of T. J.'s voice sinks in and he realizes his brother is not here to pound him. He's in way too good a mood.

"You're just in time!" Reed's mother says, her whole face brightening as T. J. bounds into the room. He shrugs out of his bulky jacket and throws it over the back of a chair, then crosses the room to his mother in one big stride, planting a kiss on top of her head.

"'Sup guys?" T. J. says, lifting his chin in the direction of the table as he plucks a slice of cucumber out of the salad bowl on the counter.

"You're in a good mood, man," Jeremy says, taking the

76

words right out of Reed's mind as T. J. munches on his cucumber and grabs a piece of broccoli.

"Why shouldn't I be?" T. J. asks, glancing at Reed with a grin.

*He knows. He knows and he's just faking his happiness to torture me,* Reed thinks, still gripping the chair. *Why else would he look at me?*

Then he notices the vulnerable glint in T. J.'s eyes, behind the over-the-top joy, and realizes with a pang to the heart that his brother is thinking of Karyn.

"No reason," Reed says, just to let his brother know the Karyn story is not public knowledge. T. J. gives Reed a quick nod and then continues to steal bits of food from various containers, telling his mother how great everything is as if she'd cooked it herself. Reed watches his brother and his mom, marveling not for the first time at the obvious strength of their connection. T. J. would never admit it, but he is a total mama's boy. And when it comes down to it, he'd probably be coming home this often even if he *did* still have regular classes. Especially now that he's suffering through a breakup. He needs his mom and his comfort food.

The protector needs to be protected.

"So, honey, what's going on with the starting position?" Reed's mother asks. "When are they going to make it official?"

Reed grips the chair with both hands now, staring down at the plate in front of him.

"It's got to be this week or next," T. J. says with a grin. "They're gonna have to announce it officially at some point. I can't wait!" He crosses to the refrigerator and pulls out a soda, popping the top as his euphoria fills the room. "It's been a tough couple of weeks, you know? I don't know how I'm gonna do on my finals and with Karyn and all. . . ." He trails off and looks at the floor and Reed can see his brother gathering himself. When he looks up again and takes a slug of his soda, the smile is back. "I'm just glad I have something to look forward to, that's all."

Reed's mother walks over to T. J. and reaches up to give him a kiss on the cheek, holding his face with both hands. "I'm so proud of you, honey," she says.

T. J. turns about ten shades of red and shoots an embarrassed look at Jeremy and Reed. "Thanks, Ma," he says.

Reed's had just about all he can take.

"I'm gonna go wash up," he says, bolting from the room before he gives in and looks at Jeremy. He can *feel* his friend's eyes boring into his skull. Telling him to say something. Telling him that keeping it a secret is not going to help his brother. But Reed doesn't know what else to do.

*Just ignore it,* he tells himself as he bounds up the stairs two at a time. *Ignore it and it'll go away. Those BC guys will take the hint eventually. They'll have to.*

Reed goes into the bathroom and quickly washes his hands, then splashes some cold water on his face. He blindly gropes for a towel and then scrubs his cheeks with it—hard. He looks up at himself in the mirror, trying to steel his resolve by staring himself down.

"Just ignore it, man," he tells himself under his breath. "It never happened. They never called. It's not an option."

Feeling better, Reed goes back to his room to grab a sweatshirt and sees that the light on his answering machine is blinking. He freezes for a second, but then he shakes his head at himself and scoffs. What are the chances?

He hits the play button. Waits for the beep. Hears the voice.

"Reed? It's Cushman—"

Reed's hand darts out and he hits the delete button before he hears another word. Then, shaking, he lowers himself down onto the edge of his bed, watching the machine warily as it rewinds and beeps.

Apparently ignoring the situation is not an option.

•••

*Okay, chew, stupid.*

It's Tuesday night and Karyn has apparently forgotten how to eat. She and her mother are sitting on top of pillows on the floor in the living room, the TV blaring *Entertainment Tonight*. There are five open containers of Chinese food from The Cottage littering the coffee table—all of Karyn's favorites—yet she keeps finding herself staring into space with a half-chewed mouthful of rice and her jaw motionless.

*Chew and swallow. It's not that hard.*

Karyn forces down the vegetable fried rice and picks up another forkful. It's interesting, really—the fact that she can't seem to concentrate on the simple act of eating just because of the voices in her head. She keeps hearing Reed yelling at her, overlapped by T. J. telling her he loves her just before he—

"Karyn? Can you pass me an egg roll?"

Karyn absently lifts her hand and gives her mother the container.

T. J.'s voice: *"You're breaking up with me? What are you—"*

Reed's voice: *"How could you do that to him? Who do you—"*

"Karyn? Hey! Are you in there?"

Karyn blinks. Swallows the latest lingering mouthful of food. Looks at her mother, her eyes stinging.

"What's up?" Karyn asks.

"You tell me," her mother replies, perfect eyebrows arched. "I asked you for an egg roll and you handed me this." She holds up an almost empty container of rice with a spoon sticking out of it. The light from the overhead lamp glints off the spoon like a twinkling star.

Karyn laughs in a strained way and shakes her head. "Sorry," she says. She picks up the egg rolls and passes them to her mother. But her mom is watching her now in that way she does when she knows something is going on and is trying to figure out exactly what that something might be. Karyn studiously focuses on her plate to avoid her mother's probing gaze, but suddenly the sight of food makes her ill.

"Karyn, is everything okay with T. J.?" her mother asks, putting the egg rolls down on the table without taking one.

Damn, the woman has talent. No wonder everyone says she's such a good guidance counselor, despite everything that's wrong in her own life. Gemma once told Karyn that her mother was either psychic or had the mind of a seventeen-year-old. Karyn's pretty sure it's the latter, and it's always bugged her that her mother acts like a teenager.

Although Ms. Aufiero actually seems to have meant that promise she made to Karyn last week. She hasn't been out on a date since Karyn got back from Boston on Saturday. Not that Karyn's holding her breath, but at least it's a start. And maybe—maybe it means Karyn *can* tell her what's wrong. She's needed to tell someone so badly, and she knows none of her friends would be able to get it. If she doesn't spill the truth to someone, she's going to explode.

"Okay, don't get mad . . . ," Karyn says, pushing her hands into the floor and shifting to face her mother.

"Oh, it's never good when people start conversations that way," her mom says. She picks up the remote and mutes the TV, then looks at Karyn steadily. Karyn can tell this is taking effort, however. Behind the calm facade, her mother is nervous. She can tell by the way her fingers are fluttering slightly as she lifts them to her temple. Her mom seems to notice this as well, pushes her blond hair behind her ear as if that was why she lifted her hand in the first place, and puts her elbow up on the couch beside her.

She rests her head on her hand, stopping the fluttering.

"Okay, hit me," her mother says.

Karyn takes a deep breath, looks down at her hands in her lap. She wants to look her mom in the eye when she says this, but she can't seem to raise her chin again, so she tells her hands instead.

"I had sex with T. J. this past weekend," she says. As it comes out, it seems to bring all the nervousness with it in a rush. The tension flows out of her body and into the atmosphere. She risks a glance at her mom.

"Oh, Karyn," her mother says, glancing away for a split second as she sits up straight. There's disappointment in her voice. Not that Karyn's surprised. And now she understands. She wishes she didn't, wishes that so badly. But she gets what her mom meant last week when she admitted during one of their blowout fights that she'd made mistakes with men, then said it was why she didn't want to see Karyn go down the same path.

*How did I do it? How did I convince myself that sleeping with T. J. was the right thing—the way to escape being a mess like my mom?* When it came down to it, Karyn had done exactly what she hated watching her mom do. She gave herself to someone she didn't love just to hide from what she really felt.

"Mom, please don't be mad," Karyn says. Almost whines. She feels like an eight-year-old version of herself. But she can't handle another argument right now.

"I'm not, Karyn. I'm not mad," her mom says, finally

looking her in the eye as if Karyn's plea has brought her back to her senses. But she looks tired. Really, really tired. "It's not like I didn't know this was coming," she says. "And I'm glad you told me. At least I know you were safe," she says wryly. But her eyes are questioning.

"Of course we were safe," Karyn assures her.

"Good," her mother says, the relief almost tangible. "And after everything that happened last week—everything we *talked* about . . ." Her mom shoots her a look, acknowledging the fact that most of those talks were, in fact, arguments. "After all that, I know you didn't take this decision lightly."

Instantly Karyn's eyes fill with tears. She's so grateful that her mother is staying calm, even though she's obviously thrown—that she's keeping her emotions in check and being the mother Karyn needs instead of freaking out. That she's here, eating dinner with Karyn and not out with some guy. And suddenly all Karyn wants to do is confess. Tell all. Before she knows she's even opened her mouth, she's spilling the whole story.

"I didn't! I didn't take it lightly, but Mom, I think I did the wrong thing. I mean, we broke up." The moment she says this, the tears start to flow, spilling down her cheeks. She fumbles for one of the coarse napkins from the take-out bag. "I broke up with him the next morning because it just didn't feel right, you know?" She looks at her mother, whose eyes are wide with sympathy. "And he was so . . . *so* hurt and I feel so guilty and . . . and lonely. And he hates me and Reed hates me and I just—"

Karyn's mother slides around the table and wraps one arm around Karyn's shoulders. The sobs grow louder the moment her mom touches her, and Karyn leans her head into her mother's shoulder and just lets it all go. For a few minutes she doesn't think about anything but feeling.

She just wishes she could make this heavy-heart thing go away. Erase the guilt. Erase the image of T. J.'s confused, devastated expression from her mind forever.

Finally, when her crying starts to die down a bit, Karyn lifts her head and blows her nose. Her mother pulls back and looks at her and the moment Karyn is able to focus, her brow wrinkles in confusion. Her mother looks . . . proud.

"Why are you looking at me like that?" Karyn asks, grabbing another napkin.

"I just can't believe how strong you are," her mother says with a small smile. She reaches out and gently pushes Karyn's long blond hair behind her ears.

Karyn chokes out a laugh. "Oh yeah. Really strong," she says, wiping under her eyes. Did her mother not just witness her insane breakdown?

"You are," her mother says, placing her hand on top of Karyn's. "You were brave enough to look at the situation with T. J., realize it wasn't right, *and* break it off. Do you realize the kind of guts that takes?"

Karyn looks down at their hands, her eyes brimming again. She doesn't *feel* brave. She just feels miserable.

Besides, how brave is it to break up with someone, hoping deep down that his brother will be there to catch you? But her mother doesn't know how Karyn feels about Reed. She wonders how much respect her mother would have for her if she found out *that* little detail.

"I know *I* would have taken the easy way out and just stayed with him," her mother continues. "Better to be in a bad relationship than be alone," she says with a sad look in her eyes. She gives Karyn's hand a little squeeze. "What you did was very strong. Don't sell yourself short."

Karyn sniffles. "Thanks, Mom," she says, utterly exhausted.

She leans back against the couch and her mother seems to take the hint that Karyn is done talking about this. At least for now. As her mom gets up and starts to clear the dishes, Karyn thinks over her mother's words. It's ironic, actually. Here her mother is, commending her for having the strength to be alone, when all the while, this whole thing was about not ending up on her own. And when she broke up with T. J., even after the way Reed had treated her last week, she'd had some small hope that they could work it out. Now that she knows beyond any doubt that he really is the one she loves, not T. J. Now that she's made the ultimate sacrifice in order to admit it to herself.

Of course, that hope is gone now, after the scene in the gym yesterday.

Karyn sighs and looks up as her mother returns from

the kitchen. They smile at each other and Karyn sits up slightly. Maybe there is something to this standing-on-her-own thing. Maybe she does need some time alone. She still doesn't want to be like her mom, always needing a guy around no matter what.

*So maybe I don't need Reed,* Karyn thinks. Then she gets up, trying to ignore the wound that opens in her heart at the mere thought of life without her best friend.

• • •

Jane clears her throat as she sits down at the kitchen table on Tuesday night, questioning her own sanity. She's sweating with nervousness and she hasn't changed out of her school clothes, hoping on some level that if she's in a button-down shirt instead of sweats, her parents will take her more seriously. Now, however, she's sure she has stains under her arms, and the last thing she's worried about is being taken seriously. She's more concerned that her whole family emerge from the impending conversation in one piece.

Her mother, at the head of the table to Jane's left, seems to feel the need to be as small as humanly possible. Her arms are wrapped around herself, her legs are crossed, and Jane can practically *feel* the muscles in her mother's body coiled and ready to spring. The woman may be small and look harmless, but Jane knows that if she or her father says one thing that tweaks her nerves, she'll lash out like a woman possessed.

Her father, on the other hand, seems as relaxed as can be. As if he's invited over to his ex-wife and daughter's house every day to chat. He's pushed back in his chair lazily, his hands folded in his lap, his eyes betraying nothing as he rolls a mint around in his mouth, clicking it against his teeth. Jane takes no comfort from his calm, however. This is how he thinks he'll get the upper hand should an argument break out. Stay emotionless. Let the women get hysterical and then come off as the reasonable one.

Jane takes a deep breath. What could possibly have made her think that talking to them both at the same time would make this easier? All she's done is unwittingly set the stage for World War III.

"Is it hot in here?" Jane asks, pushing up the sleeves of her shirt.

"Jane, I don't mean to be blunt, but can we get on with this?" her father asks. "What did you want to talk to us about?"

*Just do it,* Jane tells herself, ignoring the fact that her heat index has gone up another ten degrees just from the sound of her father's voice. She knows he hates being at her mother's house—the house they all used to share—and would like to get out of here as quickly as possible. Luckily she has a speech all worked out. If she can just stick to the speech—

"We're waiting, Jane," her mother says.

"Okay," Jane says, before either one of them can needle her any more. "I just wanted to let you guys know that I've made some decisions about my extracurricular activities."

Her parents shoot each other unreadable looks, then glance quickly back to Jane.

"I've decided to drop Academic Decathlon, math team, marching band, National Honors Society, the volunteer orchestra, Young Entrepreneurs, and French club," Jane continues firmly, looking first at her mother, then her father. Luckily they seem stunned speechless, so Jane is able to continue. "That means I still have jazz band, the Web site, *and* work, and I think that, along with cramming for the SATs, is a fair amount of stuff for me to do."

The silence at the table is suffocating, but it only lasts a moment. Then the shells start to fall.

"Jane, have you lost your *mind?*" her father says, apparently forgetting all about his stay-calm strategy. Not a good sign. "You're the president of the French club!"

"And your season with the orchestra is almost over," her mother puts in, sitting forward. "What's the point in quitting now?"

"And you can't just leave the Academic Decathlon team in the middle of the season," her father says, leaning in farther than her mom. "How are they supposed to replace you that quickly?"

With each new argument, Jane's posture sinks just the slightest bit. All of her logic starts to flit out the window. There *are* only a few weeks left with the orchestra this season and her father is right—she doesn't so much care about the pain it would be for Ms. Motti to replace her, because the woman is evil, but what about her friends on the team? She'd be letting them down, too.

*Come on, Jane. You made these decisions for a reason,* a little voice in her mind calls out. *Stick to your guns. Be strong. Be firm.*

"And what about tennis in the spring?" her father asks. "I suppose you're going to quit that, too?"

"No," Jane says, thinking this will make them back off. Her parents had always thought tennis was very important because it rounded out her applications. "I'm not quitting the team."

"Oh, well, of course not," her mother spits back sarcastically. "Because tennis is fun—"

"But it's *fine* for you to drop Academic Decathlon," her father puts in. "Something you actually have to *work* on."

"Have you ever seen me after a tennis practice?" Jane blurts incredulously. "I can't even *walk,* let alone breathe. Coach Brooks makes us do more stairs than the track team and—"

"Oh, *please,* Robert, you're the one who insisted she take tennis when she was four years old and made her go to the courts every weekend," her mother explodes, standing and pushing her chair back so hard, it hits the wall with a bang. It's as if Jane hasn't even spoken. "How dare you sit there and—"

"Oh, because her time would have obviously been *much* better spent learning another instrument," her father says, rising as well. "The glockenspiel, perhaps?"

"Don't you take that tone with me. You have no right to come into *my* house—"

"I have every right. I pay for it, don't I?"

"You unbelievable—"

As Jane's parents continue to argue, Jane sinks farther and farther into her chair. A familiar sensation crowds in around her shoulders, pressing her down. Maybe she doesn't have to drop anything. She's been doing this for four years and she's always handled it. And now she's had a little break. Maybe she can go back to it now. Maybe everything will be fine. Orchestra will be over in a few weeks and AD only meets twice each week. . . .

Yeah. Maybe she doesn't have to drop anything. If it will stop the yelling . . .

• • •

Peter wheels his chair to the edge of the porch, looks up into the star-filled sky, and smiles. This is the life. It's an oddly warm, windless December night and the world around him seems entirely peaceful. The world always seems entirely peaceful when Peter is looking at the stars. That's probably why he loves the sky at night so much and always has.

He can get lost in the sky quite easily, imagining exactly how far away the great balls of light are. Imagining some bizarre being on some foreign planet gazing out at the sun and wondering how far away *it* is. In moments, Peter is star hopping, exploring far-off worlds and forgetting all about the realities of this one. He forgets about his parents blankly watching TV inside, forgets about his lifeless legs, forgets about school and Meena and Danny and Karyn and

Reed and Jane and Jeremy.

For a moment, Peter is gone.

Then a car pulls onto his street, flashing its headlights in his eyes, and Peter is beamed back to earth. He squints at the car to see if he recognizes it but doesn't. It's some kind of station wagon mom-mobile. Peter is about to refocus on his daydreaming when the car stops a few houses down and turns around. He watches as it pulls up in front of his house and the engine clicks off.

He couldn't be more surprised when Reed Frasier gets out of the car. Reed himself seems surprised to be there. He stands uncertainly, holding his keys, the door yawning open behind him as if he needs it to be ready in case he wants to jump back in and peel away.

"Hey," Peter says.

"Hey," Reed answers. "What're you doing?"

"Nothing," Peter says. "You?"

"Just driving," Reed replies, looking off down the road. He glances back at Peter with a question in his eyes.

"You wanna come up?" Peter asks.

"Cool," Reed says. He slams the door and walks up the front path, then lowers himself onto the steps, just to Peter's left. He lets out a noise that's somewhere between a sigh and a groan and pushes his baseball cap up to his hairline, exposing his forehead. Then he leans back on his elbows and blows out another sigh.

"Okay, I may be way off here, but is something wrong?"

Peter asks.

Reed chuckles, tilts his head, and glances up at Peter. "Just one of those nights, you know? I had to get out of my house."

"I know the feeling," Peter says with a quick laugh.

Reed looks around at the porch, the flower boxes in front of the windows, then settles back down again. "Man, I haven't been here since—"

In the split second, Peter's mind is flooded with images. Jane crying. Reed and Jeremy holding hands. Flashing lights.

"Yeah," Peter says, knowing neither one of them wants to finish the sentence. "So what's going on?" he asks, hoping conversation will keep the images from coming back.

"I've got problems, man," Reed says, rubbing his forehead with his palm. "And they just keep getting bigger."

*Of course you've got problems,* Peter can't help thinking. *After all, you're here.* And isn't Peter the new Falls High after-hours advice guru?

There's a prolonged silence and Peter looks up at the stars again, listening to Reed's breathing, wondering if he's going to elaborate. Then Reed suddenly sits up, turns to lean back against the porch railing, and jams his baseball cap down again.

"I don't know what to do about Karyn," he blurts out, shoving his hands into the pockets of his varsity jacket.

Peter's eyebrows knit together. "What do you mean? Are you talking about that fight you had yesterday?"

"Kind of," Reed says, staring at some random point on the ground. "God, I feel like such a jerk for freaking out on her, but if you knew what she did—" He stops himself and shakes his head. "Actually, it's not about what she did. Not entirely, anyway."

"No offense, man, but you're not making any sense," Peter says lightly.

Reed lets out a laugh. "I know. Trust me. I know."

"Do you . . . *like* Karyn?" Peter asks.

"Yeah, kinda," Reed answers.

"Okay, then. I can see how that might be a problem." Peter knows it's hard enough to tell a girl you want to go out with her. He can't imagine what it would be like if your brother happened to be in love with the same girl.

"I know, right?" Reed says.

"So . . . what were you guys fighting about yesterday?" Peter asks, confused. "I mean, not that I'm an expert, but I'm thinking screaming at a girl doesn't exactly put her in a lovin' mood."

"I know," Reed says, shaking his head. "It's just . . . it's a long story. I was just so mad. . . . I just, I don't *get* her lately, you know? She just does these things and then she says these other things. . . ."

"Yeah." Peter pushes his palms against his thighs to warm his hands and give himself something to do as he thinks this situation over. He registers the fact that he doesn't feel his hands against his legs, but for the first time, it's more like a dim recognition than a shock to the system.

*I'm getting used to it,* Peter thinks. *That's weird.*

"Well, from what I overheard yesterday, she broke up with T. J., right?" Peter asks, glancing down at Reed.

"Yeah, but that doesn't change anything," Reed says. "Or maybe it does . . . I don't know." He looks up at Peter and Peter can actually feel the confusion in his eyes. "She kissed me last week."

"So? That's good! Maybe that's why she broke up with T. J.," Peter says.

Reed's face clouds and he looks past Peter's chair. "Yeah, but if that's true, then why—"

"Why what?" Peter asks after a few silent moments.

"Nothing," Reed replies. He takes a deep breath. "Forget it."

Peter can tell from Reed's tone that something else factors in here. Something else adding to the confusion. But if Reed doesn't feel like he should tell Peter about it, Peter's not about to push.

"Look, if she broke up with T. J., at least that means she's decided she doesn't want to be with him anymore," Peter says. He pulls back on the left wheel of his chair, turning himself to face Reed. "I know it doesn't mean that T. J. doesn't want to be with *her* anymore, but . . . well, it has to be a load off, anyway, right?"

Reed shrugs one shoulder. "I guess. . . ."

"Don't get me wrong. I'm not suggesting you just

swoop in there and ask her out or whatever, but I can tell you one thing," Peter says. "Life is too short not to go after the things you want."

Peter's words hang in the air for a moment as Reed pulls his hands out of his pockets and crosses his arms over his chest. The longer the silence prevails, the more uncomfortable Peter grows. Maybe he said too much. Or maybe he just sounded too Oprah. Maybe all Reed wanted was for him to be a guy and say, "Screw her. Who needs her?"

But that isn't in Peter. Not anymore. And he has a feeling that even if Reed *thinks* he wants to hear those words, that isn't what he really *needs* to hear.

"Ya think?" Reed says finally, looking up at Peter with a little glint of hope in his eyes.

"Trust me, I know," Peter says with a smile.

"Oh . . . right," Reed says, glancing down at Peter's chair. He pushes himself up off the ground and slaps at the back of his jeans. "I guess I should get going."

"Yeah. I'll see you tomorrow," Peter says.

"Yeah," Reed answers. He pauses on the bottom step and half turns. "Thanks, man."

"No problem," Peter answers.

As he watches Reed get into his car and drive off, Peter shakes his head. This is just getting weirder and weirder. First Jane gets assigned to help him around school, then Meena runs to him after the fire, then Danny defends him to Mr. Boyle and Karyn shows up at his house out of nowhere. He and Danny are starting to become friends again, and he and Jeremy and Reed have been hanging out. And now Reed is making pit stops on his porch.

It's like that dream he had is slowly coming true. That dream that left him feeling like he's supposed to help these people. These specific six people. And here he is, in all their lives again after being away from them for so long. He's not totally sure if he's *helping* them in any way, but until recently, he'd never known they all had so much going on. He'd never imagined he would be a person that people would confide in.

Leaning back in his chair again, Peter looks up at the stars and thinks of the warmth. He'd been just on the verge of giving up when he'd first felt it. And now . . . now it seems like the warmth is what has given him the strength to keep going. If not for that odd, comforting sensation, he might not be here right now. He might never have become close to these people again.

The warmth has given him the strength to be there for his friends. And it's going to give him the strength to walk again. He's sure of it.

# CHAPTER SiX

**"You're doing it** again," Jeremy says to Reed on Wednesday afternoon after a particularly brutal football practice.

Reed glances at Jeremy out of the corner of his eye, then returns his attention to the trophy case.

"I know," he says.

He's aware that Jeremy has a million questions, but his friend simply folds his jacket over his arm and leans back against the Plexiglas next to Reed, saying nothing. It's a comfortable silence, and Reed lets it hang for a moment. He stares at one of the pictures of his brother, arms raised in victory, football still clutched in one hand. He can't see T. J.'s face through the helmet, but he knows if he could, he would see a wide, elated grin. Reed can practically hear the roar of the crowd.

"Listen, man, I wanna say thanks," Reed says finally. He reaches out his hands, presses his fingertips to the glass, and pushes himself away, turning to face the blank wall across the hallway.

"For what?" Jeremy asks.

"For not . . . you know," Reed says, crossing to the other side of the hall. He pulls his cell phone out of the front pocket of his jeans and hits the power button to turn it on, then quickly goes through the motions of checking for missed calls. There are none. He lets out a little sigh of relief. No calls from T. J. or his mother. He faces Jeremy, who is framed by the trophy case. "For not getting on me about . . . what you overheard the other day," Reed finishes, his cheeks growing warm.

"Well, I can't say I'm not confused," Jeremy says.

Reed's jaw clenches and he hears his teeth grinding together inside his skull.

"You see these trophies? These awards?" Reed says, lifting his chin toward the trophy case.

Jeremy glances over his shoulder, then looks back at Reed like there's nothing more important behind him than a brick wall. "Yeah," he says.

"Well, these things mean everything to my brother," Reed says, crossing the hall once more and coming within inches of the glass front of the case. "He's the golden boy. The athlete. The hero. I can't take that away from him."

"But Reed—"

"Don't you get it?" Reed snaps, his eyes flashing as he turns to his friend. Jeremy doesn't even flinch, which surprises Reed because he feels like he's about to explode. "This is all T. J. has. It doesn't matter to me." He realizes

98

the falseness of this statement and swallows hard. "Not as much, anyway," he says, looking through the glass at his brother's portrait. The one that appeared in the local newspaper when T. J. won Athlete of the Year.

"I get that," Jeremy says, turning and leaning his shoulder against the glass. "But you have to know that if you turn BC down, they're just gonna find someone else. Some schmuck from Arkansas or Texas or something. They've already decided T. J.'s out."

"You don't know that," Reed says, even though he knows it's true.

"We both know that," Jeremy says firmly. He sighs and glances away, obviously considering whether to say what he's about to say. Part of Reed wants to walk away. Not give him the chance. But something makes him stay. Some part of him wants to hear the arguments. Any and all arguments that would make it okay for him to do it. To go after what he wants.

"Listen, man, I've known you for a long time, and I've never known you to put yourself in front of anyone else. Ever," Jeremy says, his gaze boring into Reed's temple. "It's something I've always admired, to tell you the truth. But sooner or later, you're gonna have to put yourself first."

Reed's jaw clenches and unclenches, clenches and unclenches. He can't put himself first. Not in front of T. J. Not after everything he's done. After all the abuse he's taken. All the times he's stood between Reed and god knows what.

"Just meet with the scout," Jeremy says lightly, as if it's the easiest thing in the world. "It's just a meeting. It's not like you're signing anything, right?"

"You don't understand," Reed says with a scoff, tipping his head forward as the truth presses in all around him. The truth that's never been spoken aloud. Not even in his own house. "I have to . . . protect him. I owe him that much."

"Protect him?" Jeremy says, incredulous. "From what? If he's not playing well, that's his fault, not yours. You can't protect the guy from himself."

*You don't get it,* Reed thinks, shaking his head. *You can't possibly understand everything that T. J. has done for me. Everything he suffered through to save me. The bruises. The broken bones . . .*

Reed closes his eyes and turns his back on the trophies again.

"Look," Jeremy says. A door slams behind them and they both jump slightly. Reed had forgotten there was anyone else left in the school. A few guys from the team file out of the locker room, and they acknowledge Reed and Jeremy as they walk by but keep going, obviously sensing there's heaviness going on here.

"Look," Jeremy says again when the others have gone. "It's not like I know everything, but I do know this—sooner or later, your life is going to have to become your own. If there's one thing I've learned from everything that's happened this year, it's that you have to be true to yourself."

"You sound like a self-help book," Reed says with a small laugh, trying to break the serious vibe.

Jeremy doesn't laugh, however. He just looks disappointed. "Come on, man. What do you really want?" he asks, his brown eyes piercing. "For you, not for your brother. Not for your family."

*Life is too short not to go after the things you want,* Peter's voice says inside Reed's mind.

Reed suddenly remembers that feeling. That high feeling he'd momentarily experienced after scoring the touchdown on Saturday. For the first time, he lets himself imagine what it would be like to have that feeling all the time. Lets himself imagine the glory, the elation, the adrenaline rush of success.

God, he wants that. He really, really does.

"See?" Jeremy says with a grin.

"What?" Reed asks, startled.

"You were smiling," Jeremy says, pushing away from the wall. "What were you thinking about?"

Embarrassed, Reed runs his hand over his mouth. For a moment, he keeps his bottom lip pinched between his thumb and forefinger, then he pulls his hand away and nods.

"I'm thinking, it's just a meeting," Reed says with a smirk. "It's not like I'm signing anything . . . right?"

• • •

Meena stares down at Holly's phone number in her planner, written in purple ink in Holly's loopy handwriting. She's been staring at it for at least five minutes, frozen between trepidation and resolve. She knows what she has to do, but she's terrified to do it. She reaches out her fingers and runs them over the writing as if just touching it can bring her back to the day it was written. That sunny summer day when Holly had received her information packet from Skidmore, complete with P. O. box address, dorm assignment, and phone number and Holly had grabbed Meena's planner to write it all down so that they would be sure to stay in touch.

Meena hasn't used the phone number in months.

*It's time,* she tells herself, picking up the phone. It's surprisingly easy to do, considering how long she's been avoiding it. She quickly goes over her script in her mind—the words she's practiced over and over again. The lies that are so much easier to tell than the truth. Then she squeezes her eyes shut in an attempt to block out the reality. To block out his face, his stubble, his touch, his skin, his smell.

The phone rings once and she almost hangs up. Twice, and the receiver is halfway to the cradle. But then a voice comes out and it's too late.

"Hello?"

Meena brings the phone to her ear. "Hey . . . Holly?"

"Meena! What's up?"

"Not much." Her fingertips squeeze into the phone so hard, it hurts. "I was just—"

"Guess where I just came from! Steven Clayton's office!" Holly says giddily.

Meena's stomach lurches and she bends forward, resting her forehead on the cool edge of her desk. Her breathing is labored but quiet, so that Holly won't hear.

*Why is this happening? How can this be happening?*

"I was calling about that, actually," Meena hears herself say.

"About what?" Holly asks.

"About . . . Steven," Meena says, lifting her head and clearing her throat. She pushes her long dark hair away from her face, then picks up a pen and starts to draw on a blank piece of paper on her desk. Jagged, blue lines. Over and over and over again.

"Oh, well, Steven *loves* you!" Holly says.

The pen goes right through the paper.

"What do you mean?"

Did he tell her? Did he tell Holly everything? Why would he do that? Why after telling her not to tell anyone would he tell her best friend? What does Holly think of her? Why is she even talking to Meena if she knows everything?

"Oh, he told me about how you baby-sit for Trace all the time and how great and sweet and responsible you are," Holly says. "You'd think he was talking about a saint, Meena, I swear. And he told me all about the fire and how you saved Trace. How come you didn't tell me about that?"

Meena's mind is reeling so fast, she's not even aware that she's been asked a question. She can't believe that Steven actually sat there and gushed about her to Holly as if all she is to him is a baby-sitter. After everything that happened, after everything he's done and threatened to do, how can he just casually talk about her like it's nothing? Like she's still the same Meena who started to baby-sit for his son months ago. Why would he talk to Holly about her at all?

"Well, whatever," Holly says when Meena doesn't answer her question. "He was so sweet when he was talking about you, Meen. He's so sensitive. He obviously cares about people, you know? Older men are so much . . . I don't know. . . . He just made me realize that the guys I date are such *boys*."

Meena's teeth bite into her bottom lip. Holly has just answered her question. Why would Steven talk to Holly about Meena at all? To make her like him. To make her think he's this incredible, sensitive man.

To start the seduction.

And it's working. It's obviously already working. Holly's voice is so thick with admiration and giddy with puppy love, it makes Meena want to puke.

"Meena? Are you still there?" Holly asks.

"Yeah," Meena says, her voice harsh. She swallows and it hurts. Her throat is so dry, she could have been running in a windstorm.

*He's so manipulative,* Meena thinks, the realization hitting her like a wrecking ball as her free hand clenches into a fist.

*How did he get me? What was his first line to me?*

"So . . . wait . . . you said you called to talk about Steven," Holly says slowly. "What's up?"

Meena walks to her bureau and stares at her reflection in the mirror that's propped up above it, steeling her eyes.

*It's time,* she tells herself, suddenly more resolved than ever. *Remember the script.*

"Well, I just wanted to tell you . . . I know Steven pretty well," Meena begins, turning away from her reflection. *Too well.* "And . . . I just don't think he's the kind of person you want to be working for."

There. That sounded good. Concerned yet disinterested. Removed.

"Really?" Holly says, her interest piqued. "What do you mean?"

"Oh, you know, he's kind of anal," Meena says, pacing around her room slowly. "You should have seen his library at home. Everything alphabetical, nothing out of place. And don't even get me started on his temper. You do one thing wrong and forget about it."

"Huh. I don't see that at all," Holly says.

*You wouldn't, because it's not exactly true,* Meena thinks. And even if it were, Steven would hide it. He's good at hiding things.

"Trust me," Meena says, closing her eyes as she stops in the middle of the room. She crosses her fingers and hopes against hope that this works. "He's not the ideal boss."

Holly chuckles. "Well, who is?" she says. "I'm not going to pass up an opportunity like this just because the guy is anal."

Meena's heart falls, fast. "But Holly—"

"Do you know how often they give these positions to freshmen?" Holly continues, sounding defensive. "Never. I'm the first one. How can I pass that up?"

*He probably chose her* because *she's young,* a little voice in Meena's head shouts out. *He likes them young.*

Meena winces at her own thoughts, disgusted and suddenly feeling dirty. As dirty as she did in the days after their first kiss. "Holly, you have to listen to me."

"Hey, Meena? If I didn't know you better, I'd think you were jealous," Holly says, a bite in her voice now.

*Jealous. Jealous. If only she knew how ironic that statement is.*

"Thanks for the warning, Meena. I have to go to dinner now. My roommate is waiting. I'll talk to you later."

"Okay . . . bye."

Holly hangs up and Meena stands there for a moment, listening to the dial tone, listening to the warring voices in her mind.

*He's so manipulative. . . . Likes them young . . . What line did he use on me . . . ?*

And then one weak voice starts to grow, drowning out the others as it swirls to the front of her mind.

*It's not my fault. It wasn't me. It's not my fault. It's not my fault. It's not . . .*

Meena slowly lowers herself onto the edge of her bed. Is it really possible? Could she actually be blameless? No.

No. She had made him want her. She had a crush on him. She'd started this . . . right?

Closing her eyes, Meena lies back and a tear spills out the corner of her eye, sliding in a warm trickle down the side of her face. She's so confused, she doesn't know which way is up anymore. But she does know one thing—whether what happened between her and Steven was her fault or not, it doesn't matter at this moment. All she knows is that she has to save Holly. She has to keep it from happening to her friend as well. She just has no idea how to do it.

• • •

"So, you look ridiculously happy," Quinn Saunders says as he drops into the chair across from Jane at Chasen's Bar and Grill on Wednesday night.

*I am,* Jane thinks, blushing. *I am because I'm with you. Perfect, handsome, brilliant you.*

She still can't believe it. She's on a date with Quinn Saunders. Quinn Saunders, who she followed around like a robotic puppy all through her freshman year. Quinn Saunders, with his floppy blond hair, his amazing blue eyes, his broad shoulders, his lovely musky scent that takes her back to late night Academic Decathlon sessions and the wide-eyed, elated innocence of a girl given the supreme privilege of hanging out with the older crowd. The cooler crowd.

"Really?" she says, ducking her head behind the leather-bound menu.

"I could get a sunburn from the sheer smile wattage,"

Quinn says with his so-cute-it-should-be-illegal smile. He grabs a carrot slice from the veggie dish the waitress has placed in the middle of their table and pops it in his mouth. "Can I take this to mean the summit meeting with the parentals went well?" he asks, raising his eyebrows.

Jane's high-watt smile fizzles and dies. "Not exactly," she says.

"Uh-oh," Quinn returns. "What happened?"

Jane tilts her head, looks at the table, the carrots, the beer menu. Anywhere but at his eyes. "Well . . . I'm thinking I might need to . . . rethink some of the things I was thinking about dropping."

"Seriously?" Quinn blurts, surprised—concerned.

Jane risks a glance at him and, yes, he actually looks concerned. How is this possible? How is it possible that Quinn really cares about her well-being? What alternate universe has she stepped into and can she please, please stay?

"They made some valid points," Jane says unconvincingly.

"Don't let them do this to you," Quinn says, looking her directly in the eye. "You can't back down."

"It's just a few activities," Jane says with a shrug.

"Yeah, but it's not," Quinn says, pushing his menu aside. "If you don't stand up to them over this, they're going to control you forever. Believe me, I know."

Jane studies Quinn's earnest face for a moment and remembers everything he said at the party Friday night.

How tough it had been for him to finally say no to all the pressure but how great it was when he did.

"It's just . . . it's really hard," Jane says, looking away. Her parents hadn't even listened to her. They hadn't waited to hear her reasons before jumping down her throat, then jumping down each other's. The yelling had gone on non-stop until Jane had agreed to rethink things. She can't do it again. Just the thought makes her shoulders tense.

"You want hard, try taking twenty credits of Ivy League classes you can't stand," Quinn says with a smirk.

Jane smiles uncertainly. "Yeah, but you don't know what my parents are like—"

"I have an idea," Quinn says. He sighs as if he's trying not to think about something and slouches back into his chair. "If I hadn't stood up to my parents, I'd be at Stanford right now, crying into my premed books. Instead I'm taking a couple of months off and then going to Australia. Not a bad trade-off."

"Somehow I don't see you crying over your home-work," Jane jokes.

"Oh, believe me, biophysiology can reduce even the best of us to blubbering fools," Quinn says. Then the spark in his eyes turns serious and he reaches across the table. He pulls Jane's hand toward him gently and lifts her fingers, lacing his through hers. For a moment, her heart stops beating entirely. "But I don't really want to think about that right now," he says. "I'd much rather just enjoy being here with you."

*Okay,* Jane thinks blissfully. *I'll do anything. Anything you say.*

At that moment, the waitress appears, knocking Jane out of her reverie. Their fingers part and she folds her hands in her lap as the waitress runs through the specials.

Jane shakes her head ever so slightly, laughing at herself. She's not actually going to do whatever Quinn says, but she is glad they talked about this. He knows what she's going through and he's brought her back to reality. It's so amazing to be with somebody who understands—who's been there. Someone who knows that it's not easy being the class overachiever.

And he's right. She can't just back down at the first sign of adversity. She's got to make sure she's doing what she wants—what's best for her—not what her parents think is best. Because it's become abundantly clear to her over the past few weeks that contrary to popular belief, adults are not always wiser. Not her parents, not her teachers, not her guidance counselor—none of them.

Jane places her order and settles back into her chair, resolved to have a good time tonight. Her father is coming over again tomorrow for further discussions, so she has until then to decide exactly what she wants to say.

For now, she's going to be New Jane. Fun Jane. And in moments, the SPF-worthy smile is back.

● ● ●

"This place is dead," Reed says, bracing his hands on the counter at TCBY and hoisting himself up on top of it.

The assistant manager, Rory Pantalone, is up to his elbows in the chocolate yogurt dispenser, cleaning it out even though it's still twenty minutes to closing.

It figures that the one time Reed needs a distraction, business has been slow. It's given him way too much time to think about what he's about to do, and his nerves are on full alert. It's also given him time to think about . . . other things, too. Jeremy isn't the only person who's given him sound advice lately, and Reed's thinking he should really listen to Peter, suck it up, and apologize to Karyn tomorrow. See if there's any chance they can still be friends, at least. If he can still breathe by tomorrow, that is, seeing as he's on the verge of hyperventilating right now.

Rory steps down from the plastic step stool, shoves his arms under the spout in the sink and turns it on full blast, then sniffs and looks at Reed. "I'm gonna go out back for a smoke," he says, a straggly lock of brown hair falling over his eyes.

Reed's heart pounds extra hard and his hand instinctively goes to his front pocket and the carefully folded piece of paper that's been burning a hole in his jeans all night.

"You sure?" Reed says, his voice coming out a little high-pitched. "It's freezing out there."

"An addict's gotta do what an addict's gotta do," Rory says with a shrug. He disappears into the tiny office behind the counter, and through the square window in the top of the door, Reed sees him grab his tattered jacket and head out the back exit.

111

Reed's eyes dart to the phone on the wall next to the sink. This is it. His one chance. It's now or never. He's spent the last couple of hours putting off the call because Jane was still here working and he hadn't wanted her to overhear anything. But after Jane left, he'd been stuck alone with Rory and, while he couldn't care less what Rory knows about his life, the guy has a rep for earning points with Peggy by reporting any and all indiscretions. Like long-distance phone calls.

Of course, that didn't stop the guy from taking twenty smoke breaks a shift.

"What am I doing?" Reed says aloud, shoving himself away from the counter.

He pulls the tattered piece of paper out of his pocket and unfolds it gingerly. It's partially eaten away on the edges because he's been playing with it all day, but the number he had gotten from the Boston College operator is still clear. Michael Cushman: 617-555-0311.

His hands are shaking.

*You have to do it now or you'll never do it,* Reed tells himself. If he calls from home, his mother will either overhear him or ask him about the call when she gets the bill. If he calls from here, Peggy will either never notice or she'll ask him about the call, make him pay for it, and tell him never to do it again. He'll take five minutes of pissed-off Peggy over a lifetime of the cold shoulder from his mother any day.

Glancing behind him, Reed quickly picks up the

phone from its cradle and dials in the number. He holds his breath, waiting for the machine to pick up.

*Two seconds. Leave a message and it'll be over in two seconds.*

"This is Cushman."

*What!*

Reed almost drops the phone. It's ten o'clock at night! What the hell is this guy doing in his office?

"Hello? Anyone there?"

"Uh . . . Mr. Cushman? This is Reed Frasier." He's holding the phone to his ear with both hands now, the scrap of paper crumpled between his palm and the back of the mouthpiece.

"Reed! I was beginning to think you were the kind who never returned phone calls!" Whatever the man says, he doesn't sound at all surprised to hear from Reed.

"Yeah, well, I was wondering if you still wanted to . . ."

*You can still hang up. End this now. Get out of it.*

"To meet," Reed says, glancing at the door to the office. He just hopes Rory goes for two cigarettes instead of one.

"Of course! Of course!" Cushman bellows. There's a squeak in the background and then the flipping of pages. "In fact, I've just had a cancellation for tomorrow night. How does that work for you?"

*Tomorrow night? Is he kidding?* Reed had thought he'd leave a message, wait for Cushman to get back to him, have some time to adjust to what he was doing before he actually had to do it. But tomorrow—

"Reed?"

"Uh . . . tomorrow sounds . . . fine," he says.

*What am I doing? Hang up! Hang up!*

"Great! I'll come down there and take you and your coach out to dinner," Cushman says. "I like that Fedorchak. Good man."

"Uh, yeah, but I don't know if he's going to be able to do it on such short notice," Reed says.

*Good thinking!* he tells himself. *That's the perfect out.*

"Oh, he'll come, trust me," Cushman says with a gravelly chuckle. "I'll give him a call. You just leave it to me."

Reed swallows. "Oh. Okay."

The back door slams and Reed's heart hits his throat. He has about five seconds to figure a way out of this before it's a done deal *and* Rory snags him and asks him who he's talking to.

"All right, then. I'll see you tomorrow night. I'll have your coach give you the details in school tomorrow," Cushman says.

Reed opens his mouth, but all that comes out is an indistinguishable grunt. It doesn't matter, anyway. He's already listening to the dial tone.

# CHAPTER SEVEN

**Karyn strolls around** the corner on Thursday afternoon, takes one look down the hall, sees Reed standing next to her locker, and immediately ducks back around the corner before he can see her. She doesn't think about it; she just does it. And the moment she realizes what she's done, she's embarrassed beyond belief.

Glancing around, Karyn plasters a confused, searching expression on her face, as if she's looking for someone who's just called out to her. Then, seeing no one, she tosses her hair behind her shoulders, presses her lips together, and starts for her locker again, confident that no one witnessed her little scared-rabbit routine. Her heart is playing jump rope in her chest, but from her cool demeanor, no one in the hallway would ever be able to tell.

Reed notices her when she's about two feet from her locker and pushes himself away from the wall to face her. Karyn, however, can't even bring herself to meet his eyes.

She gets close enough to him to smell him but ignores his presence as she starts to spin the dial on her lock.

*Oh, real mature, Karyn,* a little voice in her mind chides her. But she can't help it. She has no idea what to say to Reed. Not only is she completely confused about how she feels about him, but the last time they spoke, he ripped her to shreds. Is that what he wants to do again? Right now? In the middle of the hallway?

She misses the last number on her lock, swears under her breath, and starts all over again. Reed is just watching her. Just standing there, breathing down her neck, watching her. Can't the guy take a hint?

"Did you want something?" Karyn asks finally, dropping her lock in frustration and daring to glance up at him. "Another big chunk of my pride, perhaps?"

"Karyn, come on," Reed says gently, clutching the strap on his backpack. "Aren't you even going to let me apologize? I feel—"

"Oh, *you* feel!" Karyn says, shaking with nervousness. She somehow manages to get her locker unlocked and slams the door open into the wall. "You want to apologize to make yourself feel better? Well, that's just fine." She reaches down and pulls at her gym bag, which is, of course, stuck. She has to wrestle with it to get it out, and by the time it slides free, hurtling her halfway across the hall, she's pink from exertion and angry adrenaline.

"Karyn, calm down," Reed says. "I just—"

"I don't want to calm down, Reed," Karyn says, dropping her bags on the floor. Her arms feel heavy and she raises her shoulders, then feels herself slump as she lowers them. "Do you have any idea what I've been through lately?" she asks, looking him in the eye for the first time. "I mean, do you really think I just broke up with T. J. for no reason? That it wasn't a hard decision? That I don't feel like crap about it every single second of every single day? Do you even care that my whole life went insane last week?"

Reed blinks and the unmistakable shadow of guilt crosses his face. He looks at the floor.

"No. None of that matters to you," Karyn continues. "You just decided to use me as a punching bag without even hearing my side of the story. You assumed the worst about me. And you're supposed to be my best friend."

Her voice gets all thick and watery on the last few words and Karyn feels a breakdown coming on. Part of her wants to wrap her arms around Reed and just cry and let him hug her and tell her he's sorry. Part of her wants to smack him across the face for making her feel this way. Instead she just grabs her stuff, slams her locker, and sidesteps around him. He doesn't follow. She doesn't look back.

• • •

"I like this place," Peter says as he pulls his chair up to the round wooden table where Meena's already sitting.

"Yeah. My dad used to take my brothers and me here for Father's Day when we were too young to make him

117

breakfast in bed," Meena says, cupping her coffee mug with both hands and letting the warmth from the hot liquid soothe her nerves.

She's brought Peter to Geoffrey's because it's not exactly a Falls High hangout and she doesn't want to bump into anyone from school. It had seemed like a good idea at the time, but now that they're nestled at a corner table, she remembers what they're here to talk about and she wishes she could be anywhere else.

"So . . . I'm guessing the conversation with Holly didn't go all that well," Peter says. He twists his hot chocolate mug around and around in front of him and Meena watches the white swirls the marshmallows make as they melt.

"Yeah. It didn't work," she says, absently sipping at her coffee. "She thought I was jealous or something." She remembers Holly's voice—Holly's excited, happy voice—and it sends a chill down her spine.

"What next?" Peter asks, stopping his mug and taking a sip.

Meena shakes her head slightly to knock herself out of the little trance the marshmallows had put her in and looks at Peter. "I don't know. I don't know what else I'm supposed to do," she says.

*You can always tell,* her mind reminds her. *You can always tell the truth.*

Meena clears her throat and ignores the voice. It's not an option. Telling is not an option.

"Well . . ." Peter slowly shifts in his seat as if he's not

sure whether he should say what he's thinking. When he does, he says it to the sugar dispenser in the center of the table. "Maybe nothing will happen. Maybe Holly will just be Steven's assistant and she'll do her work and go home and everything will be fine."

A little, tiny light of hope warms Meena's chest. "You think so?" she asks.

"It's possible," Peter says, raising his eyebrows. "Anything's possible, right?"

*Maybe. Maybe he was only attracted to* me, Meena thinks again. *Maybe this* isn't *a pattern. Maybe I really am the only one that Steven . . . that Steven . . .*

She can't even finish the sentence in her own mind. She focuses her attention on stirring her coffee, unsure of whether the thought that she may be Steven's only teenage conquest makes her feel better or infinitely worse.

*It should make you feel better,* the little voice in her mind tells her as she rips open another sugar packet just so that she'll look like she's doing something. *It should make you feel better because it would mean that Holly is safe.*

But it would also mean that it really was Meena's fault. That there really is something in her that told Steven it was okay. That made him come after her.

Taking a deep breath, Meena fixes a weak smile on her face. "You're right," she says. "I could just be worrying over nothing."

"How great would that be?" Peter says hopefully.

"Pretty . . .

The "great" falls silent on Meena's tongue as the breath is taken right out of her. At that moment, while Meena watches like she's witnessing a train wreck, Steven Clayton and Holly Finneran walk into the coffee shop. He holds the door open for her and she ducks under his arm. Laughing. Giggling. Batting her eyelashes up at him.

"Oh . . . my . . . God," Meena hears herself say. Her voice seems very, very far away. She pushes herself farther into the corner, farther away from the light, but she can't stop staring. This can't be happening. It can't be.

Peter turns his head to see what has Meena so freaked, and when he looks back at her, there's fear in his eyes.

Meena watches them. Steven's hand on the small of Holly's back as she orders. His laugh. His eyes looking at Holly like she's the only girl in the world. Holly grabbing Steven's wrist as he pulls out a few bills, insisting he pay. Holly's blush when she finally accepts. The half smile. The patented half smile.

*"Older men are so much . . . I don't know. . . . He just made me realize that the guys I date are such boys."*

Meena is numb. Numb, powerless, and helpless. She feels like she did the night that Steven raped her.

Holly turns away for a moment to get something out of her bag, and the moment her back is to Steven, his whole face changes. He looks Holly up and down slowly and his eyes glint. Meena knows what he's thinking and it makes her blood curdle.

Moments later Holly and Steven have their coffees—to go—and he ushers her out of the shop. Meena finally breathes again, but it's actually painful.

"Are you okay?" Peter asks, pulling himself as close to the table, and to her, as humanly possible.

"I can't do this," Meena says, her fingers scratching at the velvet seat on either side of her. "I can't. I can't let him—"

"It's okay," Peter says, reaching out a hand toward her arm.

"No! It's not!" Meena snaps. Peter's hand withdraws, his expression startled, and Meena drops her head forward, letting her hair blanket her face. God, she hates this. She hates being this way, feeling this way, knowing what she knows.

"I'm sorry," she says quietly. Then she forces herself to look up again, and Peter is watching her openly. Patiently. "I just . . . I can't let anything happen to her."

Peter nods, silent, and Meena takes a deep breath, steels herself, and looks at the door through which the happy couple has just disappeared. For the first time in a long time, she feels resolved—determined. She feels more solid than she has in weeks.

"I can't let anything happen to her," she says again. "If it does, I'll never forgive myself."

• • •

Jeremy hasn't felt this nervous sitting down to dinner in his own house since the time he left his brand-new ten-speed behind his father's car in the driveway and his dad backed over it. Bike trashed. Fallout explosive. That night, his father had managed to get through the entire meal without saying a word, saving the psychotic learn-some-responsibility tirade for just before dessert. Tonight it seems he is going to break that silence record.

*It's the first time he's seen you in weeks,* Jeremy reminds himself. *Give him a chance.* Of course, it's not Jeremy's fault they haven't seen each other, but for the moment, he's trying to let that fact slide.

"So, Jeremy, how's school?" his mother asks brightly, passing Jeremy a large bowl of mashed potatoes. She's still dressed in her suit from work, her hair pulled back neatly and her makeup freshly applied. It all makes Jeremy feel even more like company instead of a member of the family.

"It's fine," Jeremy says, glancing across the table at his father. He's chewing, looking down at the tablecloth (the good one, only brought out for special occasions), his elbows on the table and his hands clenched together, with his fork sticking out toward his mouth. "I . . . uh . . . I think I'm getting a B in math this marking period and I got an A on my last creative-writing project."

His father lets out a snort. Jeremy turns the color of the rare roast beef on his plate as his mother darts a look at his dad, mortified. Jeremy's father never approved of the choice of creative writing as an elective. He said he didn't see how it would help Jeremy in the future.

*Just ignore him,* Jeremy tells himself. But it's hard. His father is such a presence. Not just his body, but his personality. Even when he's not talking, his father dominates the room. If the man is laughing, the whole room laughs; if the man is calm, the whole room chills; if the man is angry, the whole room seethes.

"Um, what about you, Emily?" Jeremy says, slapping some potatoes he probably won't be able to force himself to eat onto his plate. "How's school?"

"Good!" Emily says, looking warily from her father to her brother and back again. "Dad, tell Jeremy what Mrs. Marx said about my reading."

Jeremy glances at his father again, his stomach turning. His sister is too smart for her own good. And too sweet for words. His heart swells at the fact that she wants to make the two men in her family talk, but he's sure his father doesn't appreciate getting a nudge from the ten-year-old at the table.

"She said Emily was well in advance of her classmates," Jeremy's dad says, taking a sip of his water. He half smiles at Emily. "She's reading at an eighth-grade level."

"That's great, Em," Jeremy says with a smile. Emily beams back at him. Man, if only he could just talk to his sister all night, everything would be fine.

"We miss you at the halfway house, Jeremy," his mother says. "Everyone does."

*Great,* Jeremy thinks. *As if there's not enough tension here, now I have to worry about how my old job is missing me.* He finds himself wondering if he's the only one who's missed. If Josh still works there. If they fired his butt for kissing their son. Would his parents do that? Jeremy realizes that he's not so sure they wouldn't. Not anymore.

"So, Jeremy."

His heart drops so fast, it feels like it's been shoved into the floor. Is his dad really addressing him? With a wary glance at his mother, Jeremy clears his throat and looks at his father, waiting.

His dad pushes his food around on his plate a bit, mashing his vegetables into his potatoes before speaking again. When he does, he goes back to the clenched-hands pose, looking at Jeremy over the top of his fists.

"How is it, living with the Frasiers?"

Jeremy sighs. That's a loaded question. If he says it's great, his mother will be upset that he's happy living away from home. If he says it sucks, his father will probably feel somehow vindicated since in his mind it's all Jeremy's fault that he's not living at home.

"It's . . . you know. . . ." Jeremy shrugs and picks up his dinner roll, pulling off a piece and popping it into his mouth. "It's fun. Reed and Mrs. Frasier have been great. . . . I have my own room. . . ." He glances at his mother. "I miss your cooking, though," he says with a grin. "That woman keeps all the takeout places in town in business."

Jeremy's mother laughs and his grin widens; he's happy to have come up with the perfect answer. His father, however, doesn't let his steely exterior crack, and Jeremy refocuses on his food.

"And how's the team?" his father asks.

"Good. We're in the semifinals," Jeremy says.

*As if you care.*

"And, uh, Tara?"

Jeremy nearly chokes at the mention of his ex-girlfriend. He grabs his drink and swallows down half the glass to get the piece of bread lodged in his throat moving again.

"I hear she's fine," he says through a cough, his eyes burning.

Noticing his discomfort, Jeremy's mom reaches out and gently touches his dad's arm. "Tony—" she says in a soft, warning tone.

"Well, then, what have you been doing in your . . . free time?" his father asks awkwardly.

Jeremy's face burns crimson. *Don't let him win. Don't let him win.*

"I think you mean to ask, have I been seeing Josh in my free time, don't you, Dad?" Jeremy spits out, his nostrils flaring slightly. His hands are braced against his thighs, ready to push himself up and out of here in a split second.

His father's face goes ashen and Jeremy wonders if he was wrong. Maybe his dad really was asking an innocent question. But it doesn't matter. It's still clear that even the mention of Josh's name has made his father squirm.

"Jeremy—"

"No, Mom," Jeremy says, cutting her off. "I haven't seen Josh in weeks, okay? Are you relieved?"

They all look down at their plates. Including Emily. Emily, who doesn't even really know what's going on here. Suddenly all the pain comes rushing back to Jeremy like poison arrows to the chest. All the pain he'd felt the last time he was here. When he'd walked out the front door, unsure of whether he was ever coming back. Unsure of whether his parents cared about him anymore.

Tonight, apparently, he's getting his answer. They didn't want Jeremy to come to dinner. They wanted the old Jeremy to come to dinner. The one that had lived a lie for his entire young life.

"I'm outta here," Jeremy says, rising. "Thanks for dinner, Mom." He crosses over to Emily and kisses her on top of her head. His hand falls on her shoulder and hers automatically reaches up to touch his. His heart almost breaks at the tiny gesture. "I'll call you," he says.

Jeremy grabs his jacket and turns to go, berating himself for even coming here. What had he been hoping for? An apology? It would have been a start. But he'd been kidding himself if he thought—

"Jeremy." His father's voice calls out over the sound of a chair scraping across the floor.

Jeremy stops, clutching his jacket in his fist. The silence fills his pores.

"Just . . . wait. Don't go," his father says quietly. So quietly, Jeremy isn't totally sure he didn't say it in his own mind. That it isn't wishful thinking.

Slowly he turns around. His father is standing in front of his plate, the fingertips of one hand resting on the table.

"Look, I . . . didn't mean anything," Mr. Mandile says, his voice flat, as if he's worried if he lets any emotion in, it will be the wrong one. "I'm not good at this."

"Good at what?" Jeremy asks. His father's always been good at handling every situation in the book. What's so incredibly different now? He's had weeks to make a move—to get over his initial surprise and realize that Jeremy is still Jeremy.

"This," his father says, swallowing hard. "Admitting I'm . . . that I'm wrong. That I don't know how to handle something."

Jeremy holds his breath. He's afraid to move or speak. They're all hanging by a thin thread here and if anyone says the wrong thing, the small step his father just made could be erased.

"Look, all I know is that I don't want to lose you, Jeremy," his dad says. "I'm sorry about everything I just said, everything I said before. That's what I really want to say. That I'm sorry."

Jeremy's mother and sister both turn to look at Jeremy with unabashed hope. The magic words. They've actually been said. Jeremy's head is so full of confused thoughts, it's like somebody shook up a Scrabble board in his mind.

His dad comes around the table and stands right in front of Jeremy, a couple of inches shorter but twice as broad. Jeremy can tell from the prominence of the vein in the middle of his dad's forehead that this is not easy for him.

"I'm not saying I'm totally comfortable with the way you're living your life, Jeremy, but I'm asking you to give me some time," his father says. He clears his throat and crosses his bulky arms over his chest. "Just . . . come home. We'll work it out."

Jeremy feels like he did when he was a little kid and every word his father spoke was wise and the truth. No questions asked. His father has said they'll work it out, and they will. Jeremy is suddenly sure of it.

"Okay, Dad," he says, somehow keeping himself from crying. "I'll move home."

• • •

"Dessert, Reed?"

"Yeah, I'll have the New York cheesecake," Reed says, slapping the little dessert menu closed and handing it to the hovering waiter.

"I like it," Cushman says, reaching out his arm to smack Reed, hard, on the back. "I like a guy who can eat."

"I can't help it," Reed says. He reaches for his soda and takes a gulp, shooting Cushman and his coach an apologetic glance. "I eat when I'm nervous."

Michael Cushman and Coach Fedorchak look at each other and then they each let out a deep belly laugh, as if Reed has just told the most classic joke of all time. It's all Reed can do to keep the baffled expression off his face.

Everything he has said this evening has solicited either guffaws or intensely serious contemplative expressions. He's never had two adults pay so much attention to him in his life. And he's fairly certain that this much laughter goes against Fedorchak's very nature.

"Why're you nervous, son?" Cushman says, draping his arm over the back of Reed's chair and leaning his stocky frame toward him. "Haven't I made it clear that we want you? There's no question here, kid. This date is a sure thing," he adds with a wink.

More belly laughs. Reed feels his skin heating up and is relieved when the waiter comes back with coffee. It gives him a moment to take a few deep breaths and try to come down off the high he's experiencing. All he's done for the last two hours is eat amazing food and listen to Cushman talk about the legacy of excellence he will become a part of if he goes to Boston College. He talked about striving to be the best, winning championships, integrity, tradition, honor, heart, athleticism. He's even brought personal letters from various deans, urging him to come to BC for the school's stellar academics, along with a letter offering him a full scholarship if he joins the team.

Reed has never been so seduced by anything in his life.

"So . . . why're you nervous?" Cushman asks again, taking a loud sip of his coffee.

Reed shifts forward in his seat and leans into the table. "Honestly? Because a lot of my mother's friends come to this restaurant," Reed says quietly. "I've been waiting all night to get caught."

He'd told his mother he was going over to Shaheem's house to watch the Thursday night game on ESPN. His mother hadn't even batted an eyelash. But she would be batting a few thousand if she found out where he actually was and who he was actually with.

"Get caught?" Coach Fedorchak says rather loudly. "What are you doing that's so bad?"

Reed can't believe these guys haven't figured it out yet. Either that, or they're choosing to ignore the fact that his being here is akin to driving a knife into his brother's back. And the longer he sits here and listens to them, the more he's thinking of going through with it. Of actually committing the ultimate betrayal.

"Coach," Reed says, deciding to focus on the man he and his brother have known for five years. Deciding he's Reed's best bet for understanding what he's going through. The guy has to have *some* qualms over sending a new quarterback to BC to take the place of the gridiron hero he sent there *last* year. "You have to know if T. J. found out about this—"

The lazy grin falls away from Coach Fedorchak's face and he presses his hands into the table, standing. "Mike, would you excuse me and Reed for a moment?"

Surprised, Reed scrambles to get up and follows his coach over to the little hallway that leads to the bathrooms, his heart pounding. His heart always pounds when Coach takes that move-your-ass tone with him.

"What's up, Coach?" Reed asks, shoving his hands into the front pockets of his chinos.

"What's up?" Coach repeats, actually looking flustered. He glances around him with a wondering expression as if he's asking the little old lady who's just emerged from the bathroom what, exactly, he's supposed to do with this kid.

"What's up is that you're being offered the brass ring here, Reed. And you're spitting on it!" he says, his bug eyes bulging.

"I'm not . . . spitting on it," Reed says as the tiny woman squeezes between the two of them and out into the dining room. "But Coach, I don't understand. Don't you know that this will kill T. J.? I thought you . . . I don't know, I thought you cared about him."

"I did!" Coach says under his breath. "I mean, I *do*. But Reed, I know for a fact that if you don't take this man up on his offer, they're going to keep looking. No matter what you do here, T. J. Frasier is not the first-string quarterback for Boston College next season."

Reed swallows. Jeremy was right. Of course Jeremy was right. But hearing Coach say it makes it so much more real. So much more of a legitimate factor.

*It doesn't matter,* Reed tells himself. *You can't do this. You owe T. J. your life. You can't——*

"Look, your brother . . ." Coach brings his hands to his

hips and looks at the wall above Reed's head, choosing his words. "Your brother is a great player. No one is denying it. But Reed, you are a leader. T. J. never had that quality you have on the field. That spark. You make those guys want to win for you. Our team this year has half the talent it did last year. I graduated eight all-state and five all-county players last year. Six of 'em got scholarships. There's no way anyone was picking us to go anywhere this year. But here we are in the semifinals, and you, my friend, are the reason."

The coach might as well be using a tire pump to fill Reed's head and heart. By the end of this little speech, he's floating about three inches off the ground. Maybe he does owe T. J. his life, but does that mean he shouldn't live it? Maybe . . .

"I don't know what to say," Reed tells his coach. He'd had no idea the man felt this way about him.

"Well, I can say this," Coach says, resting a hand on Reed's shoulder. "I wish I had realized this about you earlier, because I would have started you in the first game last year if I'd known what you were capable of."

Reed looks into his coach's eyes and feels a rush of confidence surge through his body. He can't imagine that he's the *only* reason the team has done well this year, but the facts *are* there. T. J. had graduated with half the starting lineup. Reed recalls, in fact, a morose afternoon late in the season last year when he and the other juniors on the team had sat around a table at the diner, lamenting exactly how badly they were going to suck this year. Instead they were dominating. Could Reed really have been responsible?

Was he actually a better quarterback than his brother?

"This is your chance, Reed," Coach Fedorchak says, looking across the restaurant at Cushman. "So few people get a chance like this. You're one of the lucky ones. Don't let it pass you by."

Those last few words sink in slowly. And suddenly Reed knows what he has to do. He knows what he's *meant* to do. There will be consequences. Big ones. But he'll deal. He has to.

This is his life. It's time to live it.

# CHAPTER EiGHT

"Mom? Mom, can I come in?"

Reed knocks lightly on his mother's door and presses his lips together as he waits for an answer. He has energy coming out of his fingertips, his scalp, his very skin, but he has to stay calm, or she's going to know something's up. And if she asks him anything, he's not sure he's going to have the self-control to keep his excitement at bay.

"Yes, Reed." His mother's voice is muffled. He pushes the door open a couple of inches and finds her sitting up on her bed with her glasses on, reading by the soft light from the lamp on her nightstand. She lays her paperback aside and looks up at him. "How was the game?"

"Good," Reed lies with a smile. He has no idea what happened in the football game. At the moment he can't even remember who was playing. "It was good."

"Good," she says. A little wrinkle appears above her nose. She's wondering what he wants. This visit during her private time is not a normal thing.

"When's T. J. coming home again?" Reed asks, still holding on to the doorknob.

"Tomorrow night," his mother says. "He doesn't have a game this weekend. Why?"

She has a suspicious look in her eye. Reed knows his mother isn't stupid. He's acting strangely—his grin is way too big for someone who has simply spent the night kicking back in front of the TV. She knows something is up.

"I just have something to tell you guys and I want to tell you both at the same time," Reed says, adding a shrug for good measure. "What time will he be home?"

"Around six." His mother pushes herself up a bit and crosses her arms over the front of her cream satin robe. "What is going on, Reed?" she asks, her eyebrows raised.

Suddenly Reed has an intense urge to tell her everything, as he knew he would. He wishes he could just say, "Mom, guess what? I'm going to be BC's starting quarterback next year!" And that his mother's face would light up. That she'd hug him. That she'd tell him how happy and proud she is. But it's such a foreign concept, Reed can't even imagine it happening. He draws a blank when he tries to.

No. Better to tell them both at once. Get it over with. Deal with their anger and hurt at the same time so he can put it behind him and get back to the way he's feeling right now. This elation.

"It's no big deal," Reed lies. "I just want to tell you guys together, that's all."

"Okay," his mother says. She gives a little eye roll at his silliness. "Good night, sweetie."

"'Night," Reed says.

He walks into his bedroom and closes the door, then stands there looking around, unable to conceive of what to do next. He's nowhere near tired. And the idea of trying to do homework is laughable. What he really feels like doing is jumping up and down on his bed, but that could cause serious structural damage.

Reed's eyes fall on the phone and he has the sudden, intense urge to call Karyn. He's had a taste of what it's like to get what he wants and now a big part of him wants it all. He wants to call her and apologize again, to tell her he wants to be with her and ask her—no, beg her—to forgive him for being so harsh when it was really *himself* he was angry at.

He takes a step toward the phone, then freezes. What is he, crazy? This is not the kind of conversation a person should have over the phone. No way, nohow. If he's going to make up with Karyn—and he is—he *has* to be able to share this with her. It's something he needs to do right.

He has no idea how he's going to do it, but now he somehow knows he can. If he can take that spot at BC, he can do anything. Right now, nothing can bring him down.

So for a moment, he just stands there, letting himself grin and feel. Because he knows that the longer he's alone, the more this feeling is going to wane. And when it wanes, it's going to be replaced by the guilt, the fear, the doubt.

Reed looks down at the framed picture of him and T. J. on his desk and sighs.

"Just get it over with at one time," he says quietly. "One conversation and it'll be over."

The problem is, he knows it's a lie. Tomorrow night's little talk will be just the beginning.

• • •

*It's time for round two,* Jane thinks as she and her parents settle down in the living room on Thursday night. Hopefully she can pull it off this time. It took enough courage just to tell her parents that she needed another "conversation," that even though she'd relented on Tuesday, there was still more she needed to say. And that she needed them to let her say it this time.

Jane sits back against the couch, but the moment she hits the cushions, she pushes herself forward again. This is no time to get comfortable.

"Jane, I'm sorry about how your father and I acted earlier this week," her mother says, crossing her legs. Jane can't help thinking that her mother looks like a therapist, sitting in the high-backed chair at the end of the couch, looking at her with that studied expression of understanding and sympathy. "We were supposed to be talking about you, and instead we . . ." She shoots a glance at Jane's father, who's standing next to the fireplace like a sentry, and he lowers his eyes. "Well, we made it about us. We shouldn't have started arguing with each other like that when there was something you needed to discuss," her mother says. "But tonight we're prepared to listen."

*Huh,* Jane thinks, a little ray of hope breaking through the clouds in her mind. *Maybe this won't be so bad.*

"Okay," she says. She takes a deep breath and stares down at the cover of the *Better Homes and Gardens* magazine on the coffee table. "Then I guess I should tell you, I haven't changed my mind." Her eyes flick up to her father, who doesn't move a muscle. "I'm going to drop the things I said I was going to drop and keep what I want to keep."

Her mother is the first to let this sink in. "Jane, I really think you're making a mistake here. If you—"

"Mom, no," Jane says. Her mother's mouth snaps shut, and Jane's heart pounds with fear over interrupting her so harshly. She decides to just keep talking. Not give her mother time to reprimand her.

"Look, I have one more chance to take the SATs—in January," Jane says. "And I think we can all agree that is the most important thing for me to do right now. If I don't do well, I'm not going *anywhere.* And it won't matter whether I was in the orchestra or on the decathlon team."

Her father pulls his arm away from the hearth and puts his hands in his pockets. He's pondering this. He's realizing it makes sense. Jane feels the ray of hope widen into a strong beam.

"I need the extra time to study and to . . . prepare myself," Jane says carefully.

"Jane, you never did tell us what happened with that

test," her mother says, sounding a bit exasperated. "As far as I knew, you *were* prepared. You did well on your PSATs, you studied. What on earth happened?"

Jane clears her throat, her mind conjuring flashes of images from that day. The empty Scantron sheet, the baffled faces of classmates, the empty hallway she'd run through on her way back to the car. She takes a deep breath and pushes it to the back of her mind.

"I panicked," Jane says, staring down at her hands. "I sat there, and I felt like I was having a heart attack. My heart was racing. . . . I couldn't breathe. . . . I was sweating and nauseous, my thoughts were all over the place and I couldn't stop it. Nothing made sense." She glances at her mother, whose face is all confusion. "I freaked and I ran. I didn't even take the test."

Stunned silence permeates the air. They're not only disappointed in her, now they think she's insane. Her father is the first to speak.

"Why would you panic, Jane?" he asks. "You knew you were going to ace it."

Jane almost laughs. "*That's* why," she says.

"What? What's why?" he asks, shrugging and shaking his head.

"That! That . . . pressure," Jane manages to say. "You guys don't just want me to do well; you expect it. Do you have any idea what it's like to get a ninety-five on a test and be *disappointed?*"

Her parents just look at her blankly. Jane realizes with a

sickening twist of her heart that they both, on some level, think she *should* be disappointed if she gets a ninety-five.

*Don't freak out,* she tells herself, feeling her anger and tension start to boil up. *If you freak out now, this whole thing will be pointless . . . again.*

"Okay. There's something I need you to do," Jane says, squeezing her hands together tightly.

Her father clears his throat. Adjusts his hands in his pockets, jangling his change. "What's that?"

"I need you to back off," Jane blurts out.

"Excuse me?" Jane's mother says, standing up. "Young lady, I don't think I like your tone."

"I'm sorry," Jane says, keeping her voice miraculously calm. "That didn't come out the way I wanted it to."

"You're telling us to *back off*?" her mother rants, as if she hasn't heard Jane. "We're your parents, Jane. I'm not even sure I know what you mean."

"I *mean,* I can't take the pressure anymore," Jane says, her voice growing louder as she glares up at her parents. "You guys are always on top of me, telling me what to do, when to do it." She stands up, partly because she's bursting with anger and partly because she feels small, gazing up at them from the couch.

"*You* tell me that this is more important than that," she says to her mother. "Then *you* tell me that *that* is more important than *this,*" she adds, looking at her father. "I never even have time to think for myself. I don't even know what

I want anymore because my head is so full of *your* voices, telling me I have to do this, I have to go there, I have to ace this, I have to practice and study and work and fulfill my obligations. I can't take it anymore!"

For a moment they just look at her like they don't know who she is. Jane decides to take the opportunity to plunge forward. "From now on, I need to make my own decisions. I'm going to be deciding what's important and what's not."

She glances at her father, whose eyes look tired. He seems broken somehow. "I hope you guys will be there for me, but if you aren't . . . well, I guess that's *your* decision."

For a moment, Jane stands there, waiting for more. Knowing there will be more arguments, but they don't come. Neither do any apologies. Any words of understanding.

"Well, I have to go study," Jane says, sapped of all energy. She turns and walks out of the room, feeling very sorry for herself.

But when she gets to the stairs, she lifts her foot to the first step and freezes as a realization suddenly washes over her. She's never heard her parents so quiet before. They're not calling after her with demands. They're not yelling at each other, playing the blame game. From what she can tell, they're not even moving.

And that's when she knows she's finally gotten through to them. She's finally made them think. She smiles and climbs the stairs to her room.

• • •

"Look! I made it in art," Emily says, crawling across her bed and snatching a large piece of paper that's on the bedside table, propped up against the wall. When Jeremy had told her he had to get back to the Frasiers' after dinner, she'd insisted he come upstairs for a few minutes, and he'd been more than happy to oblige. He hasn't been in Emily's room, or his own, in weeks. She hands the paper to Jeremy and sits on her knees on her bed, waiting with a smile for his reaction.

Jeremy looks down at the swirls of color. "It's beautiful, Em," he says, handing it back to her. "What is it?"

"It's abstract," she says with a little tongue cluck, as if she feels sorry for him and his artistic ignorance.

"I see that," Jeremy says, letting out a little laugh. He looks around her brightly colored room, which, for the first time ever, is actually pretty tidy. Jeremy wonders when Emily started cleaning up her room. He hadn't thought he'd been gone long enough for anything to change.

"What were you and Mom and Dad fighting about?" she asks suddenly, pulling him back with a fierce yank at his heart. "I keep waiting for someone to tell me."

Jeremy looks down at her and shoves his hands in the front pockets of his jeans. He knew he was going to have to explain this to her sooner or later, but he has no idea where to begin. The girl is ten. How much does she know about sex and love and the way the world works?

He sits down next to her on her bed and she pushes

one of her long red braids behind her back, watching him innocently, waiting for a simple answer.

"We had a . . . misunderstanding," Jeremy says, folding his hands together and resting his forearms on his thighs. "I told them something about myself and it . . . surprised them."

Emily's little eyebrows knit together. She obviously needs more.

"It upset them," Jeremy adds, starting to sweat. "But they're feeling better about it now."

"What did you tell them?" Emily asks, clearly baffled. In her world, there's obviously nothing bad enough to make their parents that mad. "Did you steal something?"

Jeremy can't help letting out a chuckle. How great it would be if that were true. If that were all he had done. Theft would probably be a lot easier for his parents to get over than the thought of their only son kissing a guy.

"No, nothing like that," he says. He pulls his leg up onto the bed so that he can turn and face her. He might as well just spit it out and explain later. He takes a deep breath and looks her in the eye. "I told them I was gay."

Emily blinks. "Oh," she says. Her face betrays nothing.

"Do you know what that means?" he asks.

"I'm not stupid," she says, rolling her eyes. "I watch *Dawson's Creek*."

Jeremy laughs and shakes his head.

"It's a good show!" Emily says indignantly, mistaking the cause of his laughter.

"Okay," Jeremy says, wiping at his eyes. "I know." He makes himself calm down. "So . . . is there anything you want to ask me?" he asks, half afraid, half curious to hear what she says.

Emily shifts her sitting position, crossing her legs in front of her Indian style, and pulls her favorite doll into her lap. She rests her chin on the stuffed doll's head and looks up at him.

"What about Tara?" she asks.

Jeremy takes the little shot to the heart. "Well . . . we broke up," he says. "But I hope one day we'll be friends again."

"Is Josh your boyfriend?" she asks, raising her eyebrows.

Another shot to the heart. "What makes you say that?" he asks, his stomach shifting as he recalls the kiss. The amazing, unbelievable kiss that had felt like his first.

"You said something about him at dinner," Emily answers.

Wow. This girl didn't miss a beat. Not that Jeremy's surprised. She's always been light-years ahead of her time.

"He's not my boyfriend," Jeremy says, looking down. "I'm not really sure what he is." It's been so long since he's let himself think about Josh, it hurts to do it.

"Well, *I* think he's cute," Emily says with a grin.

Jeremy chuckles and reaches for Emily, pulling her into his lap.

"Ah! No!" Emily cries, laughing. "Let me go, you dork!"

But Jeremy isn't about to listen to her. He hugs her

tightly and plants a kiss on top of her fiery red hair. If only his parents had been born in the nineties like Emily. It would have made the last few weeks so much easier.

"You're pretty cool, you know?" Jeremy tells her.

"Yeah, I know!" Emily responds. She squirms her way out of his lap and back to her own spot on the bed.

Jeremy stands up and stretches, taking a deep breath and letting it out slowly. "Well, I'm gonna go back and spend the night at Reed's," he says. "I'm too tired to get my stuff and come home tonight, but I'll be living down the hall again before you know it, okay?"

"'Kay!" Emily says brightly.

"Good night, Em," Jeremy says with a grin.

"Later!" she says with a wave.

He shakes his head and walks out into the hallway. Two seconds after he's gone, he hears her portable stereo flick on and some pounding *N Sync song blasts through the wall. Jeremy smiles wistfully. He knew he'd missed his sister, but he'd had no idea how much.

He leans back against the wall, listening to her sing along, and his mind wanders back to Josh. Josh and how that kiss had made him feel. It had changed everything. It had made so much seem possible. How had he let himself forget that?

But Jeremy knows how. He's had to deal with the kids at school, which he's done. Then he's had to deal with his parents, which he's done. He's had to concentrate on making his world livable again. But now that it is, now that things are getting back to normal, maybe it's time for him to deal with his feelings for Josh.

• • •

It's Friday morning, and Peter and Meena have been sitting in silence in the empty classroom for ten minutes. Ten long, torturous minutes. Ten minutes in which Peter has been constantly arguing with himself. He knows what he has to say, but he's petrified to say it. Has been since last night, when he realized there's no way around this and called Meena to ask her to meet him at school early today so they could talk. He doesn't want to upset her. Doesn't want to hurt her. He'd rather rip his own heart out than hurt her.

But it's out there. They both know it. It needs to be said. Nothing will ever be right for her again if she doesn't hear it. Doesn't act on it.

Peter opens his mouth, then closes it. He pushes his wheels back and forth, back and forth, back and forth. He's holding his breath.

"I just don't know what to do," Meena says suddenly, sitting back and then forward in the hard desk chair. "After the last conversation I had with Holly, I don't know if she'll even believe me if I tell her the truth. She'll probably just think I'm lying." She tips her head forward and disappears behind her hair. "She'll probably think I'm jealous," she adds, her voice thick with emotion and irony.

"Meena." Peter's voice sounds strange. Like he hasn't used it for days. Her dark eyes land on him, wide and full

146

of trepidation. She can tell he's going to say something that she doesn't want to hear. "You know what I'm going to say."

She pulls back slightly. "Don't."

"You have to tell your parents," he says gently.

Meena pushes her hair away from her face and looks up at the ceiling, blinking. Her eyes are glimmering with tears. She seems to shrink before his eyes.

"I can't," she says.

"They'll help you," Peter says. He pushes himself forward a few inches so that his knees are about a foot from hers. "You know they will."

Meena pulls in a shaky breath and lets it out. She looks at him out of the corner of her eye, then looks away so quickly, it's as if the sight of him has burned her corneas. Peter swallows hard.

"They're your parents," Peter says quietly. "If you tell them, they'll do something about it. And if they do something about it, then . . ."

She's looking at him intently now.

"Then chances are, nothing will happen to Holly," Peter finishes, trying to make his voice confident. Trying to keep his green eyes steady. She needs someone to be sure. And he's the only one who has a clue what's going on. So he needs to be that someone.

"What do you—" Her voice cracks and she stops and shakes her head at herself. "What do you think will happen to him if I tell them?" she asks. "What do you think they're going to do?"

"I don't know," Peter says. He pauses, summoning the guts to get it out—*the* question. "You know, Meena," he says softly. "You never actually told me. I mean—did he, did Clayton—" He stops, feeling his throat close up. "Did he rape you?"

The room is so quiet, Peter can hear his heart thumping wildly as he waits for her response, afraid he'll scare her into shutting down completely. But after a moment she gives a small, sad nod. And Peter feels his whole stomach twist.

He coughs. "Well, it, uh, it depends how your parents handle it. But I'm sure they'll report it to the police, and the police will question him. They'll definitely investigate it. They might arrest him." *They'd better arrest that piece of filth.*

Meena lets out a wry laugh, wet with tears. "I can't do it," she says.

"What do you—"

"You know what I mean, Peter," she says, more forcefully than she's said anything in the few weeks since they've started talking. "If they investigate it, they're going to ask me all kinds of questions. And if they arrest him, there will be a trial. And if there's a trial, I'm going to have to tell everything."

She pushes herself off the chair and stands, her body taut with emotion. She runs her hand over her face and pushes her hair away.

"Do you think I haven't thought about this?" she asks,

looking down at him. "It's *all* I think about. All night long. I've been through every possible scenario a million times, and I can't do it. I can't face that. I can't . . . face him."

"Yes, you can," Peter says firmly. "If you can live through what he's already done to you, you can do anything."

Meena's face registers disbelief at his conviction. She seems to think he's kidding. Peter wants to tell her how amazing he thinks she is. How strong. But he's afraid she'll realize how he feels about her. And now is not the time for that conversation.

"You have to do something about this," Peter says, pulling his right wheel back and angling his chair to face her. "You said it yourself. But it's not just about helping Holly. Steven Clayton needs to be punished for what he did to you."

"Peter—"

"I don't want to pressure you," Peter says gently. "But it's time. And I think you know it is. If you do the right thing here . . . just imagine how much better you'll feel."

Meena's face flushes and she looks away. Peter immediately feels like he's said too much. He wants to smack himself for making it sound like he presumes to know how she feels. How could he possibly know? But what he does know is that he's felt despair. He's felt guilt. He's felt it all. And the only thing that has made him feel better is helping other people. It's the only thing that has given him any sense of redemption. Made him feel worthy again.

Peter watches Meena and waits for her to think it through. He crosses the fingers of one hand and covers them with the other. At that moment, she finally looks him in the eye.

"You're right," she says. "I have to tell them. But I can't do it alone."

Peter's mouth goes dry, but he doesn't blink. He simply nods his agreement and he can tell that Meena understands. He'll be there. He'll be there for her.

# CHAPTER NINE

"I cannot believe you are going to be playing for BC next year, man," Jeremy says as Reed pulls his jacket out of his locker on Friday afternoon.

"Yeah, can I touch you?" Peter jokes, reaching out a hand and lightly pushing Reed's back.

Reed feels a little flutter in his heart and tries not to smile too broadly. Every time he even *thinks* about himself in an Eagles uniform, he feels the little heart-flutter. It's out of control.

"Just don't tell anyone, okay?" Reed asks them, glancing over his shoulder at the crowded hallway. "It's not official and I don't want it all over school just yet. I want to deal with my family first."

Peter and Jeremy exchange a wary look, and the little wings on Reed's heart turn to stone, causing his excitement to take a nosedive. The day is going by incredibly slowly. It's not like he's looking *forward* to talking to his mother and T. J. tonight, but he does want to get it over with. He hates the anticipation.

At least he and his friends are going out to lunch. Not only will it make the period breeze by, but if he's going to do his nervous overeating thing, he'd rather have it be real food than cafeteria slop. He slams his locker, checks his wallet for cash, and heads off down the hall, Peter and Jeremy trailing behind him.

"I just can't believe I'm actually going to play football in college," Reed says quietly as he shoves his wallet into the back pocket of his jeans. "I've been daydreaming about it ever since I was in the peewees, but I never thought it would actually happen."

"That's because you were never on a team where T. J. wasn't starting," Jeremy points out, glancing around to make sure no one's overhearing them. He reaches up to adjust the gold chain that has his football number, three, dangling from it. "Until this year *I* was never on a team where T. J. wasn't starting."

"I know," Reed says. His face is slowly heating up as the three of them cross the lobby. He doesn't want to talk about this anymore. It's bad enough that he can't stop *thinking* about it, but talking about it is making him feel even worse. What would T. J. do if he knew about the conversation he and his friends are having right now?

*He'd die of humiliation,* Reed thinks as he holds the door open for Peter.

"I wonder if they're going to announce it to the press," Jeremy says, his eyes bright.

"Let's talk about something else," Reed says abruptly.

They all stop just outside the doors and Peter looks up at him, clearly surprised.

"It's just—" Reed takes a deep breath and looks away. He doesn't want to explain right now. Explaining would mean talking about it even more. "Let's just talk about something else," he says again.

"That's cool," Jeremy says.

Reed shoots him a grateful look. Jeremy, at least, knows what the deal is between him and T. J., so he understands. He knows *some* of the deal, anyway.

"So, where're we going for lunch?" Peter asks, slapping his hands together.

Reed opens his mouth to answer at the exact instant that Karyn walks through the lobby doors behind Peter, alone. The moment she sees them, she looks away and lifts her chin slightly, but Reed can tell she's flushed. She's flushed just at the sight of him. Part of him wants to call after her and say something, but he has no idea how to start. And he's more than a little afraid she'll make an idiot of him in front of the guys. So he just lets her go.

How is he ever going to apologize for what he did to her? Is she ever going to let him?

"What's up with you two?" Jeremy asks.

"*There's* a new subject," Peter says with a trace of sarcasm.

Reed manages to smirk. "What's that expression?" he asks, lifting his baseball cap from his head and letting the chilly air cool him for a moment before yanking it back down. "Out of the frying pan, into the fire?"

"Sorry," Jeremy says, shaking his head. "If you don't want to talk about it—"

"No. It's okay," Reed says. He starts walking along the side of the building toward his car. "I have no idea what to do anymore. I tried to apologize, but she wouldn't let me."

"But you don't *just* want to apologize, right?" Jeremy says.

Reed stares at his boots as he walks. "Not exactly."

"Well, I'd say Karyn is the type of girl who needs to be swept off her feet," Peter says matter-of-factly.

Swept off her feet. Reed looks off across the parking lot. Thinks about T. J. He can't imagine his brother doing anything particularly gooey for Karyn. It's just not who he is. But Peter's right—Karyn loves all that romantic stuff. And so does he, though he'd never admit it within earshot of any of his friends.

*You and Karyn are right for each other,* a voice in his mind urges. And T. J. may love Karyn, yeah, but he isn't right for her. Never really was. It's just like with the football scholarship. Reed can turn his back on Karyn, on the feelings he has that it seems like she just might have, too. But it's not going to make Karyn go back to T. J.

"I don't know," Jeremy says slowly. "She just broke up with T. J. Isn't it a little soon?"

Reed cringes. It does sound pretty bad, but it doesn't *feel* too soon. In fact, it feels like he's waited forever for this moment.

154

"But hey," Jeremy adds when he sees Reed's expression. "If you want to go for it, that's your call. I've got your back."

"Thanks," Reed says with a small smile. He slides between his car and Gemma Masters's BMW and stops by the driver's side door. "Because I might need your help."

"You have a plan already?" Peter asks, narrowing his eyes. He stops behind Gemma's car so that Reed can pull out before the guys help him in.

Reed laughs. "Not exactly," he says as he unlocks the car. "That's why I might need your help."

● ● ●

*Okay, you can do this,* Jane tells herself, rolling her shoulders back as she walks ever so slowly down the hall on Friday afternoon after school. *Just walk in there, tell her you're quitting, and leave. You've done this before. You're becoming a veritable expert at saying those two words, "I quit."*

Okay, so she'd ended up rejoining the activities she quit last week. But the meetings she'd had with advisers today where she really *had* quit activities, for real, had gone okay.

*Because those teachers aren't Ms. Motti.* The Academic Decathlon adviser is going to be a different story and Jane knows it. It's why she's been avoiding this wing of the school all day.

Why has she done this to herself? She should have gotten the hard one over with first instead of dreading it all day.

"Well . . . here goes nothing." Jane stops just outside Ms. Motti's room and peeks in. She catches a glimpse of the rather large woman at the blackboard and her body seizes up with fear. She wonders if any of the teachers at this school have ever actually physically attacked a student before.

"Don't be an idiot," she says under her breath.

Then, before she can chicken out, Jane steps into the room and clears her throat, categorically certain that her voice won't work. Ms. Motti is writing the goal list for that afternoon's practice on the board and the chalk is clicking away so loudly, the woman doesn't even hear her.

*Okay,* Jane thinks.

"Uh, Ms. Motti?" she says.

The teacher finishes writing before she turns around.

"Jane! Good!" she says, stepping to her desk and picking up a piece of paper. "This is a list of books you need to review before our next meet. I don't want to have a repeat of what happened a couple of weeks ago."

She holds the paper out to Jane, who's standing clear across the room. Caught off guard by the greeting, Jane can do nothing but walk over and take the cleanly typed page. It's a bibliography of about thirty books. Jane has to concentrate to breathe.

"Now, I've listed them in order from the most important on down," Ms. Motti says, rifling through some more papers on her desk. "But don't take that to mean that the ones on the bottom aren't important, because they are. I'm going to need you to . . ."

Jane grips the page, waiting for an opening. Waiting

for Ms. Motti to take a breath so that she can get a word in edgewise. The longer the woman rattles on about strategy, the more annoyed she's going to be when Jane tells her she's quitting and she's been babbling for no reason.

Unfortunately, it seems that the woman doesn't need oxygen. Jane is finally forced to do the unthinkable—interrupt Ms. Motti.

"Um, I'm sorry—"

The teacher's eyes widen in shock and she looks at Jane, who feels like withering up right there in front of her.

"I'm in the middle of explaining something to you," Ms. Motti says stiffly.

Jane winces. "I know, and I'm sorry," she says, holding the bibliography in front of her stomach like a shield. "It's just, I came here to resign from the team."

There. She said it. She's free!

But Ms. Motti is . . . laughing.

"That's very funny, Jane," she says, nodding as she turns toward the board again. She picks up a piece of chalk and starts to write once more. "Thank you. I haven't had a good laugh in weeks."

*Try a lifetime,* Jane thinks. She comes very close to simply walking out of the room. Does she really have to say it *again?* It had taken enough effort to say it the first time.

"Ms. Motti? I . . . wasn't kidding," Jane says.

The teacher pauses with her hand above her head, the

chalk millimeters away from the board. She turns to face Jane and now her eyes are dead serious.

"You can't quit in the middle of the season, Jane," she says, bringing her arm down.

"You have plenty of alternates," Jane reminds her. "Carrie Donovan can take my place. She's been dying to—"

"Carrie Donovan is a sophomore!" Ms. Motti snaps, her voice growing louder. It seems to be finally sinking in that Jane isn't joking around. "I can't have a sophomore starting on this team."

"I'm really sorry," Jane says, her resolve starting to crumble. "It's just, I need the time to study and I—"

"Do you have any idea how irresponsible this is?" Ms. Motti shouts, her voice filling the room. "What is happening to you, Jane? How could you be so selfish as to let your teammates down like this? And with the states coming up . . ."

The longer Ms. Motti yells, the blurrier she becomes as Jane's eyes fill with hot tears. No teacher has ever yelled at her before. Ever. She's never thrown a spitball in her life. Never joked in class. Never so much as spoken out of turn. The experience is terrifying.

*Don't let her get to you,* a little voice in her mind cries out. *This is your decision. She's just a mean, bitter old woman and she can't intimidate you.*

"I'm disappointed in you, Jane. Do your parents know what you—"

"It's been nice working with you, Ms. Motti," Jane hears herself say suddenly.

Ms. Motti is just as surprised as Jane is by the strength of her own voice. But somehow, the mention of her parents has snapped her out of her miserable cowering. If she stood up to them, she can stand up to anyone.

"Good luck with the rest of the season."

Jane drops the bibliography on the nearest desk and walks out of the room, sweeping by Sumit and Regina, who are just arriving for practice. They both stare after her, but neither says a word, probably sensing the tension in the air.

As Jane strolls down the hallway, her chin lifts just a bit higher and she feels a slow grin spread across her face. Her step is as light as air. It's over. She's done it. Meet the new Jane Scott.

• • •

*Thank God there's no cheerleading practice today,* Karyn thinks as she unlocks her car door in the mayhem-plagued parking lot on Friday afternoon. She can't imagine dealing with listening to everyone talk about their weekend plans. Listening to Gemma gush about whatever exploits she and her boyfriend, Carlos, are going to be up to. All she can think about is getting home, putting her feet up, watching mindless MTV reruns, and leaving this whole painful, crazy week behind her.

She opens the car door and is halfway into her seat

when someone calls her name. Karyn closes her eyes and pushes herself up again. She was almost home free.

"Hey, Jeremy," she says with a weak smile as he jogs in front of a stopped car to get to her.

She tucks her hair behind her ears and reaches into her pocket for her lip balm. No need to look gross in front of Reed's best friend and houseguest. Much better to have him go home and tell Mr. Frasier just how perfect and not upset she looked.

"What's up?" she asks, applying a fresh coat to her lips. She stands between her open car door and escape. Maybe if she doesn't close the door, he'll take the hint and not keep her long.

"Nothing. I just haven't seen you much lately," Jeremy says, running a hand over his spiky brown hair. "I wanted to say hi."

*Right,* Karyn thinks. *And I'm Buffy the Vampire Slayer.*

"Okay, hi," she says with an accommodating little laugh. "How are you?"

"Fine," Jeremy says. He gives a little nod and he looks off toward the street, shoving one hand in the pocket of his jeans. "So, what's up with you and Reed?"

*Wow,* Karyn thinks, her stomach clenching. *He didn't waste much time pretending he doesn't have an agenda.* But that's Jeremy. He's always been a fairly straight shooter. Except for the whole radical lifestyle change.

"Nothing," she says nonchalantly. "We're just . . . not talking at the moment."

"Do you want to make up with him?" Jeremy asks.

Karyn feels her face flush and wishes she had more control over her skin. "Well, if he would stop *yelling* at me every five minutes and have an actual conversation—"

She stops herself, annoyed. So much for acting unaffected.

Jeremy looks at the ground, turns, and leans back against the car right next to her. "Karyn . . . you know I know how you feel about him, right? I mean, I think we kind of got that out of the way at the diner last week."

Karyn swallows. She doesn't have the energy to deny it, and he's right—she hasn't hidden it that well from him, anyway. "Well . . . it doesn't matter either way," she says, choosing her words carefully and watching Jeremy's reaction like a hawk. "Even if I did like Reed, he's made it pretty clear that he's not interested."

"Yeah, right. And I'm Buffy the Vampire Slayer," Jeremy says.

Karyn laughs out loud at the little mind-reading moment and her face burns. Finally she can't take it anymore. "Jeremy, is there a point to this conversation?" she asks, crossing her arms over the front of her varsity jacket.

"What if I told you I could prove that Reed likes you?" Jeremy asks, narrowing his eyes mischievously. "You do want to know, don't you?"

Karyn's heart gives an extra thump. This is insane. If

anyone had told her this would be the conversation to end this past week, she would never have believed it.

"You're not going to whip out one of those notes where he asks me to check off whether I like him or not, are you?" she asks coyly.

"No," Jeremy says with a laugh. "Are you interested?"

"Depends," Karyn says, grinning from embarrassment and at the silliness of the situation. "What are we talking about here?"

"Meet me at the Falls tonight and you'll find out," Jeremy says with a matching smile.

The Falls? Is he insane? Karyn tilts her head and studies him, but she cannot for the life of her figure out what's going through his mind.

"What?" Jeremy says, pulling himself up straight.

"Nothing. I just feel like we should be having this conversation in a dark parking lot wearing trench coats," Karyn jokes.

Jeremy laughs. "Just . . . be there at nine," he says. Then he gives her one last grin and walks off toward his car.

Karyn leans back against her car and stares down at the driver's seat, all thoughts of kicking back with Carson Daly fleeing from her mind. What is going on here? The Falls is where everyone goes to make out. It's like the foggy-car-window capital of the Northeast. The whole thing is just too bizarre.

Someone peels out of a nearby parking spot and wakes Karyn from her thoughts. She turns and plops down in her seat, slamming the door.

"I don't even know if I want to go out with Reed, anyway," she says to the windshield, her key poised inches from the ignition. Hadn't she decided it would be better to be alone for a while? Or had she merely decided that because Reed had bitten her head off, convincing her that he wasn't interested? And . . . because she still feels terrible about breaking T. J.'s heart, and maybe deep down she doesn't think it's fair for her to be happy with someone else. Especially his own brother.

Karyn sighs. T. J. hasn't called once. Hasn't sent an e-mail. Nothing, no effort to get her back or to find out why she dumped him. She's not really surprised. She knows how proud he is. But she also knows she really, really hurt him. And isn't she as bad as her father if she rushes right from crushing someone who cares about her into the arms of someone else?

"Ugh!" Karyn moans as she starts up her car. She rests her forehead against the steering wheel for a moment, mentally reviewing her conversation with Jeremy. As she does, she knows it doesn't matter whether or not she's decided to be alone, whether or not she feels guilty about T. J. Reed is as much a part of her as her own heart, and there's nothing that can keep her from the Falls tonight. She has to find out what's going on.

• • •

Reed pulls his car to a stop in his driveway on Friday evening and kills the engine. The top of his brother's SUV is visible through the tiny garage windows. T. J. is home. He and his mother are probably inside right now, discussing T. J.'s future. Discussing the Heisman Trophy and the NFL draft. Discussing events that will never happen.

Reed is more than ready to hightail it out of here. Move to another state and change his name. But he stops himself, his stomach churning. He has to do this. He has to get it over with before he gives himself an ulcer.

He walks inside and closes the door quietly behind him, then pauses in the foyer, listening for voices. Sure enough, his mother's girly laugh trills through the house from the direction of the den. Reed puts his backpack down on the floor, takes a deep breath, and walks through the kitchen to the entrance to the den. His mother is sitting on the couch, her arm slung over the armrest, laughing as T. J. animatedly relates a story in the center of the room. It takes a few moments before either one of them even notices he's there, which is odd, considering his heart is pounding loud enough to be heard three counties away.

"Oh, hey, man," T. J. says with an easy smile when he finally spots Reed hovering. "So, what's the what? Mom says you've got some big news. What'd they do, give you another egghead award?"

"Uh, no," Reed says. It's a perfect opener. T. J. picking

on him will make this somewhat easier. Barely, but it's a start. "It's a lot bigger than that."

"What is it, sweetie?" his mother asks. She has to glance behind her a bit to see him.

Reed takes a few steps into the room and looks at them. It's odd, having this knowledge that's going to change their lives. Heady and sickening all at once.

"Yeah, man, what is it. Egghead of the *year?*" T. J. laughs heartily at his own joke.

"Maybe you should sit," Reed tells his brother.

T. J.'s face twitches almost imperceptibly. Reed can almost hear him deciding whether to take his advice or not. Whether it would be cooler of him to stand. But finally T. J. sits down next to their mother.

Reed takes a deep breath and tries to swallow down his heart, but it doesn't work. There's nothing left to do but tell them.

"Well, here goes," Reed says. He unsnaps his jacket and tosses it on a chair. When he actually looks down at his mother and brother, it feels wrong—awkward somehow. Then he realizes he's probably never had center stage like this before. At least not in this house.

*Talk,* Reed tells himself. *They're waiting. Just get it over with already.*

"There's this guy from BC," Reed says, focusing on T. J. "You might know him. Michael Cushman?"

T. J. blinks. "Yeah . . ."

"Well, he . . . uh . . . called me earlier this week and it turns out they want me to come to BC," Reed says. *Okay. That part's out.*

"Seriously?" T. J. says. Simply surprised. Nothing else.

"I don't understand. Who is this Cushman person?" Reed's mother asks, her perfect brows knitting over her perfect nose.

"He's a scout for the football program," T. J. says before Reed can. A certain wary suspicion is starting to seep its way into T. J.'s eyes.

Reed's mother's face lights up like a Christmas tree. "Reed, that's wonderful! You and T. J. will be playing together again? I think that's just great!" She looks at T. J., all grins, but T. J. senses there's something else to this. He's starting to look a bit ill. Tiny beads of sweat have appeared along his hairline.

"Yeah, we are going to be playing together again, Mom," Reed says. Suddenly he can't stand anymore. He sits down on top of his jacket and squeezes the fingers on his left hand with his right. "The thing is . . . The thing is . . ."

*Say it!*

"They want me to be the starter."

It's as if someone has just dropped a thick, suffocating muffler over the room. It feels darker. Stuffier. Unbearable.

Reed looks at his brother. His face is in his hands. He isn't breathing.

"This isn't happening," T. J. says into his fingers.

"What do you mean, they want you to be the starter?" Reed's mother says, her eyes wide. She turns to T. J. and almost accusingly says, "I thought you were the starter."

"I am!" T. J. blurts out angrily, bringing down his hands. He glares at Reed, his expression a mixture of hurt and total fury. "What the hell do you think you're doing?" he spits out. "You can't start at a college level. You've never even started at a high school level."

"Uh . . . yes, I have. All season," Reed says.

T. J. blows out a breath, brushing Reed off. "One season, whatever. There's no way you're doing this. There's no way they asked you to do this."

"They did," Reed says quietly.

"This is crap!" T. J. shouts, standing up, veins bulging out of his neck, his face going purple. For the first time in his life, Reed sees the resemblance between T. J. and his father and he presses himself farther back in his chair.

"T. J., honey, calm down," Reed's mother says in a calming voice. "Reed, maybe you misunderstood them. Maybe they want you to play backup to your brother."

Reed looks into her eyes, her pleading eyes, and wants to scream. She's pleading with him—actually *pleading* with him—to take his usual place. To take the backseat. How can she sit there and do that? But Reed knew this was coming. He knew she wouldn't be able to accept that T. J. isn't going to have everything she thought he had coming to him. He has to stay calm or this whole thing is going to get even more out of control.

"I didn't misunderstand them, Mom," he says. "They want me to start. I have the letter upstairs. They're giving me a full scholarship."

T. J. throws his hands in the air and groans. He turns his back to them and walks to the far wall, bracing one hand against it and looking down at the floor as if he's trying not to throw up.

"Well, can you still turn them down?" Reed's mother asks.

"What!" Reed blurts out before he can think twice, his face scrunching up in disbelief. Now it's his turn to stand. "Are you kidding me? This is the opportunity of a lifetime. Don't you want me to do what I want to do? Or do you only care if T. J.'s happy?"

Reed's mother pales and she suddenly looks frail enough to be picked up by a strong wind. "Now, Reed, that's not fair—"

"No! It's *not* fair!" Reed shouts. He's way beyond any self-control at this point. "All you care about is T. J.! I'm your son, too, you know!"

"God, Reed, you're such a baby," T. J. says, looking disgusted.

"Oh, good argument, T. J.," Reed spits out. "Look, I'm sorry, but I'm not gonna do this anymore. I know you have a learning disability and I'm sorry about that, but I'm not going to feel guilty for being smart anymore. And I'm not going to feel guilty for being a good football player."

Reed takes a deep breath. "And I'm not going to feel guilty because you took the worst of it from Dad anymore, either," he adds, his heart slamming against his rib cage with fear over merely mentioning his father.

"Reed," his mother says in a warning tone.

"No, Mom!" Reed says, cutting her off. He's letting out years of pent-up emotion and he can't stop himself now. He couldn't if he tried. He turns his gaze back to T. J., whose arms are hanging limp at his sides. He seems afraid to hear what's coming—just as Reed's afraid to say it—but he has a resigned look in his eyes. Suddenly Reed knows that on some level T. J. realizes this needs to be said. For a moment it makes him feel like they're on the same side.

"I know you protected me when we were little," Reed says evenly. "I don't think I really realized it then, but I do now. I know you put yourself in Dad's path when he was coming after me." Reed's voice breaks and his eyes fill with tears, but he manages to swallow some of it back. Enough so that the tears don't spill over. "And I'm grateful for it, T. J., but I'm tired of feeling guilty about it. I really am."

"Enough!" his mother shouts, standing up. She has little rivers of black makeup running down her cheeks. "I will not hear your father spoken about that way!"

"We *never* talk about him in *any* way," Reed says, his eyes stinging. "And I'm so sick of it. He was an asshole, Mom. It's not your fault, but he was. We wouldn't be standing here like this if he wasn't. We wouldn't be the messed-up, twisted, dysfunctional family that we are. I wouldn't have felt like I had to wait a week and get up the guts to tell my mother and my brother the best news of my life."

His brother tips his head forward and wipes the back of his hand across his face. Reed hasn't seen T. J. cry since he was about ten years old.

"I can't take it anymore, you guys," Reed says quietly. "I can't take never saying what I want or doing what I want. And I hate feeling like this. Like no one cares about me." He takes a deep breath and blinks back the last of the tears. "I'm sorry Dad beat us up all the time, but he's been dead for four years and I'm still letting what he did control my life. I'm done with it."

Reed's mother pulls in an audible breath and uses both hands to wipe her face clean. Reed looks at her, clueless as to what she's going to say, but when he sees the steely look in her eyes, his insides hollow out.

"How could you?" she says flatly. "I can't even look at you right now."

She might as well have slapped him in the face. Reed was hoping for something, anything from his mother. One sign of love or at least understanding. He'd never expected this.

"Mom . . . please—"

"Reed," she says more quietly. She looks at the floor and covers both eyes with one hand. Her body shakes as she cries. "Please, I just . . . I can't do this right now."

She turns and hurries out of the room. Reed's heart jumps when she slams her bedroom door moments later.

Slowly he turns to look at T. J. and T. J. lifts his head. His face is wet, but oddly, he doesn't look nearly as angry as his mother did. He looks sad, and shocked, but he doesn't look angry anymore.

"I hope you can find a way to be happy for me," Reed says quickly. Then he grabs his jacket and walks out of the house before he either bursts into tears or throws up.

# CHAPTER TEN

**What is it** *about the unexpected?* Karyn wonders as she leans forward in the driver's seat on Friday night, carefully wending her way through the dark, foggy streets of Winetka Falls. Her stomach is clenched in so many crazy knots, it could earn itself a Boy Scout merit badge. And why? It's not like Jeremy is going to *do* something to her. It's not like he's anyone she should be afraid of or even expect something weird from.

So why is her heart pounding like it did before her first ever cheerleading tryout? Why does she keep thinking about turning around and going home?

"Calm down," Karyn says, taking a deep breath and rubbing her hands together against the cold as she stops at a red light.

*But it doesn't make any sense,* a little voice in her mind cries out. *Why does Jeremy need to meet you at the prime hookup spot? And what possible proof could he have that Reed likes you?*

Karyn feels a giddy smile take over her face and looks wistfully through the windshield. *Does* Reed really like her? And if so, what is she going to do about it? From the fluttery, jittery thing her heart is doing at the mere possibility, she knows how hard it would be to fight the urge to go for it. But could either of them ever do that to T. J.? The kiss was one thing . . . but a *relationship*?

A horn honks behind her and Karyn starts, glancing up to realize the light is now green. She has no idea how long it's been that way, but she slams on the gas and hangs a right. Her nerves are now entirely frayed.

Karyn grips the steering wheel as she focuses on the road ahead. There's no moon out and this particular stretch has no streetlights. The fog makes it difficult to see as she climbs the hill, and her heartbeat gets louder and louder.

Suddenly she imagines a freaked-out psycho escapee jumping over the guardrail from the bushes, brandishing a blood-covered steak knife.

It's the perfect night for it.

"Yeah. Jeremy Mandile is luring you up here to kill you. Get a grip." Karyn laughs at herself and rolls her eyes. Still, she wishes the night didn't have to be so spooky on top of everything else.

But she's almost there. As soon as she gets to the Falls parking lot, there will be at least a few cars parked. Plenty of people around and headlights on. It'll be fine.

Karyn makes the turnoff that will take her up to the lot

and the lookout. Any second now. Any second now and she'll know what this is all about. Listening to her heartbeat, Karyn knows for the first time in her life what the expression "the suspense is killing me" is all about.

She makes the turn into the lot . . . and no one's there. Not a single car.

"Okay, *now* I'm freaked," Karyn says aloud, slowing down considerably.

Where is Jeremy? Is he late? But even if he is, where is everyone else—the couples that have populated this place every weekend night since her parents were still wearing bell-bottoms?

"That's it. I'm outta here," Karyn says. She turns the wheel to the left to turn around, but just as the car starts to shift, her headlights catch on something and she distinctly sees a glint of metal.

Heart now in her throat, Karyn steps on the brake and squints into the foggy night. There's something. Something at the far end of the parking lot near the woods. A car. And someone standing near the trunk. Part of her wants to turn the wheel back again and investigate, and part of her is screaming to get the heck out of there. Nothing's worth having her throat slit by a knife-wielding madman.

There's a sudden, small flash of light and Karyn suddenly sees . . .

Wait a minute. No. It can't be. . . .

• • •

"So, Meena, what is it you wanted to talk to us about?" Meena's mother asks as she and Meena's father walk into the living room and sit down on the couch.

They look over at Meena expectantly, but Meena just stands in the doorway between the living room and the foyer, her hands pressed together in front of her. She keeps rubbing her palms against each other—hard—trying to feel something other than the overwhelming fear that's taken hold of the rest of her body.

"Uh . . . just one minute," Meena says, glancing at the front door.

Where is Peter? She can't do this without Peter. How could he be late? Tonight of all nights.

"Are you waiting for someone?" her mother asks, her forced smile fading slightly in confusion. Meena knows her mother is scared of this conversation. Was from the moment Meena asked her parents if they could talk.

*She probably thinks I'm going to tell them I'm pregnant,* Meena thinks. *She probably thinks I'm waiting for the father or something.*

At that moment the doorbell rings. Meena's mother and father both stand up as if the sound were accompanied by an electric shock to the couch cushions.

"Meena, what's going on?" her father asks.

"One second, Dad." Meena lunges for the door and opens it to find Peter sitting there, an apologetic look on his face. The force of the relief she feels almost makes her faint.

"Sorry," he says under his breath, pushing himself over the threshold.

She holds the door open for him and says nothing. Now that it's time to speak, she feels like she won't ever be able to do so again. She shakily follows Peter into the living room. Now her parents look *really* confused.

"Hi, Mr. and Mrs. Miller," Peter says, positioning himself next to one of the chairs.

"Peter Davis," Mrs. Miller says, now with a forced smile wide enough to drive a truck through. "How nice to see you." She sits down carefully on the couch, seemingly wary of another electric shock. Meena's father follows suit.

Meena hovers by the door, watching the whole bizarre scene, her hands all the while rubbing. She tells herself to walk into the room. Sit down. Do what she needs to do. But instead, her foot takes a step back.

"Meena?" Peter says, looking over his shoulder at her.

His green eyes are full of strength. Meena pulls her foot back. Keeping her gaze trained on Peter and away from her parents, she walks into the room. She manages to make it to the chair, sits down, and, without even thinking about it, takes Peter's hand.

When she glances up at her parents, they're both staring at those clasped hands.

"Whatever you're thinking right now, it's not right," Meena says, her heart pinballing around erratically. "What I'm going to say has nothing to do with Peter. Peter's here because he's been a really good friend and . . . I thought I might need one for this."

Her mother blows out a little sigh. Lifts her long brown hair off her neck and lets it fall again. Her father pushes himself back into the couch, getting comfortable. Clearly he's not as concerned as her mother is.

"Well, Meena? What's going on?" her mother asks, crossing her legs and clasping her hands around her knee, her back straight as a board.

Meena takes a deep breath and it catches in her throat. Peter squeezes her hand and she glances at him. "This isn't easy," she says.

"Meena, you're scaring me now," her mother says sternly. "I want to know what this is about."

*Okay,* Meena thinks. *Good place to start. What this is about. Small steps.*

"It's about . . . Steven Clayton," Meena says.

Peter's mouth lifts at the ends ever so slightly. She's doing it. He's proud.

"Steven?" her father says, sitting forward. Clearly this is, in no way, a name he expected to hear. "What about Steven?"

"You have to promise me you're going to stay calm," Meena says. She doesn't think she can handle her parents freaking, even though they have every right to.

"Meena," her mother says in a warning tone.

"He raped me," Meena blurts out.

Peter's grip on her hand tightens and Meena feels like his strength is the only thing keeping her from crumbling. Her parents go ashen. No one moves.

"What?" her mother says finally. It's more a breath of air than a word.

"It was over a month ago, at his house," Meena says, feeling oddly detached now that she's begun. "Before it . . . before the fire. I was baby-sitting."

"Oh my God," Meena's mother says, covering her mouth. She looks at Meena's father, her whole body seeming to cave in on itself. "Oh my God, Ethan—"

Her father blinks at the sound of his name. He leans forward, bracing his forearms on his knees, and looks at Meena. "Meena, that's a very serious accusation. I want to be sure that you know what you're saying."

Meena's eyes fill with tears. "Dad, I know," Meena says, one fat tear rolling down her cheek. "I know what he did to me."

Before Meena knows what's happening, her father has grabbed her up in his arms and her hand slips out of Peter's. Her dad is hugging her so tightly, she can barely breathe. She stands there, hugging him back, as her mother sobs.

"Don't hate me," Meena says, crying as a ball of guilt, fear, confusion, and self-loathing she's been keeping inside for all these weeks bursts open and overwhelms her. "I didn't mean for it to happen. I didn't—"

"We don't hate you," her father says into her hair. "How could you think that?"

"I'm sorry. I just—" She can't talk. She can't think. There's just too much.

"Why didn't you tell us?" her father asks, breaking away from her. He bends so that he can look into her eyes. "You're telling me this happened over a *month* ago? Why didn't you—"

"And he's been *living* here!" her mother says, her eyes horrified as the realization sweeps over her. "Meena, when he was here, did he—"

"No," Meena says through her tears. She wipes the back of her hand over her nose. "No. I thought he was going to, but I never gave him the chance, I guess. I don't—"

"I can't believe this," Meena's mother says, looking at the floor. "How could this happen? We invited him into our *home!* You're our baby and we . . . How could we . . . ?"

Meena has never seen her mother cry like this before. Has never seen her unable to get control of herself.

"Mom, you didn't know. How could you have known?" Meena says, sitting down next to her mother.

She looks up at Peter and he gazes back confidently, telling her she's doing fine. Meena reaches out and touches her mother's hand and the moment she does, her mother envelops her in her arms, still crying.

"I should have known," she says. "You've been so upset and removed and you're never here. How could I have not figured it out?"

"You could never have guessed," Meena says. "I should have told you."

Her mother pulls away and looks Meena in the eyes. She touches her face and frowns sorrowfully. "How could he do this to my sweet little baby?" she says tearfully. Then she sniffles and straightens herself up, as if she's had a sudden realization. "We're taking you to a doctor."

"Mom, it happened weeks ago," Meena says.

"It doesn't matter," her mother says, squeezing her hand. "You need to be checked. And we have to—"

"Call the police," her father finishes, his voice thick. "He's going to answer for this." He actually starts to walk from the room as if he's going to make the phone call that very second.

"Dad, wait!" Meena says, reaching out her hand.

Her father turns and looks at her, his eyes shining with tears.

"Just . . . can we just . . . sit for a second?" Meena asks.

Without a word, her father comes back to the couch and puts his arm around Meena. She's never felt so secure in her life, sitting there being embraced by both her parents.

"We're going to take care of this," her father says softly. "Don't worry, Meena. You have nothing to be afraid of anymore."

Meena takes a deep breath and looks at Peter. Her heart is filled to bursting when she sees him. "Thanks for being here."

Peter smiles and then Meena squeezes her eyes shut. All she wants to do is stay here, wrapped up like this, forever.

• • •

That night, after Mr. Miller thanks him for being there for Meena and encouraging her to come forward, then drops him off at his house, Peter feels like he's floating. He's so proud of Meena. And so impressed with the way her parents reacted. Before he'd gone to her house, he'd tried to mentally prepare himself for the worst—tried to figure out what he'd do if they didn't believe her.

But they clearly love Meena. And he knows everything is going to work out. By the time he maneuvers his way into his bedroom, Peter is feeling pretty good about the world. Something awful happened, but everything is going to be okay.

Peter pushes his chair through the door and catches a glimpse of something white and square in the middle of his bed. He wheels his way over, reaches out, and snatches the piece of paper up with his fingertips. He freezes the moment he reads it. It's a note from his mom. He has an appointment with Dr. Chang on Monday.

Dr. Chang. The person who's going to tell Peter if he's ever going to walk again.

*But I am,* Peter tells himself, shrugging one shoulder in

an attempt at faking out his irrational fear. He crumples the paper and, with a quick hook shot, launches it into the garbage can next to the door.

*But what if I'm not?* he thinks a moment later.

His stomach feels hollow as he allows himself to ponder the possibility. That he'll never feel his legs, his feet, his toes again. That he'll never get out of this chair. That he'll forever be pitied. Looked down on. That he'll always have these calloused hands, always be looking at people's waists instead of into their eyes. That he'll be a statistic. A handicapped person.

"No," Peter says aloud, pushing himself up straight. Meena had shown strength beyond reason tonight. Now it's his turn. If he lets himself wallow, he'll be betraying her in some way. Be letting her down. And that's not going to happen.

"Okay, I can do this," Peter says, pulling back his wheels and centering himself in his darkened bedroom. He closes his eyes and concentrates all his energy on his right leg. He pictures it. Sees his foot moving. Sees it shift an inch on its footrest.

"Come on," he says, gripping his armrests as his eyes squeeze even tighter. *Move. Move. Just a little. Just a bit. Come on. Move. Move, move, move, move, move!*

Peter starts to sweat. Feels little rivers running from his temples along his face. *Feel something. Anything. An itch. A chill. An ache. Anything.*

He's holding his breath. He's pushing himself so hard his muscles have tightened to the point of pain. But nothing's happening. Nothing's changed. Peter can't feel a thing.

He releases it all—his hands, his eyes, his breath—and looks down at his legs. A small sob escapes his throat.

"Dammit!" he says under his breath.

*It's never going to happen,* a taunting voice teases. *You're kidding yourself. All this time you've been so sure, but it's not going to happen. You're stuck. You've got wheels. Live with it.*

Peter hangs his head and presses the heels of his hands into his eyes. This can't happen. He can't be stuck like this forever. Not after everything he's been through. Not after coming together with Jane and Karyn and Meena and Reed and Danny and Jeremy again. Not after the dreams.

He'd thought he was being redeemed. He'd thought he was being forgiven for what he'd done.

*You'll never be forgiven,* the voice says. *How can you ever be forgiven for that? You committed the ultimate sin. You took away something so precious—*

"No," Peter says, crying now. "I didn't mean to. I didn't know. I just want to walk again. I just want to—"

Peter stops in the middle of his ranting when he feels a warm sensation touch him in the middle of his forehead. It rapidly spreads, emanating like ripples in a pond, over his entire body. His neck, then his shoulders, then his arms and torso and fingertips. With each inch of skin it envelops, Peter grows more and more calm. More and more serene.

Everything is going to be fine. His confidence returns and the despair he'd felt just moments before is like a fading memory.

He's fine. Meena's fine. They're all fine. And Peter will walk again. He knows it with a certainty beyond anything he's known before. He will walk again. And then he will know that he's finally been forgiven.

• • •

Reed looks up at the pitch-black sky and says a little "thank you" when Karyn finally kills the engine and the headlights. She's only been idling for a minute, but it feels like hours. He quickly glances one last time over the spread set up behind the car. Nice thick blanket to sit on, check. Tablecloth, check. Candles, check. All her favorite foods from Phil's, check. His dad's old camping heaters, check. Now all he has to do is stop shaking like a leaf and everything will be fine.

Maybe.

*Bag it,* Reed's conscience, which is sounding a lot like T. J.'s voice, tells him. *You've already devastated your brother once tonight. What are you going to tell him if this little romance works out? You've got the scholarship. Do you really need the girl, too?*

Karyn is slowly approaching through the fog. Reed's blood is racing through his veins and his heart is pounding against his ribs. What is she going to do? How is she going to react?

And then she steps into the light. Reed takes one look at her broad smile, her shining eyes, her gaze of wonder as she looks around, and the last question his conscience posed is answered.

Yes, he does need the girl. In fact, he needs the girl more than anything else. He'd give up the scholarship if it meant he could have the girl. That's how much this beautiful, amazing best friend of his means to him.

"Hi," Reed says, pushing his hands into his pockets. His heart is pounding in anticipation. "Surprised?"

"Are you kidding?" Karyn says, glancing down at the setup. "What's going on?"

"I . . . well . . . a lot is going on, actually," Reed says.

She glances at him out of the corner of her eye. "How did you do all this?"

Reed's shoulders relax slightly. He's relieved to have a story to tell. "Well, Jeremy and Peter and I sort of spread the word at school that they were repaving the Falls lot tonight so no one would show." He looks around at the deserted parking lot. "I guess it worked."

"And . . . why did you want to meet me at the Falls?" Karyn asks.

"Because it's the only romantic spot in this entire town," Reed says with a grin.

An unmistakable spark comes into Karyn's eyes, even as she seems to be fighting to keep the rest of her expression even.

Reed knows that spark. It's all the encouragement he needs.

His heart thumps once so hard, he's sure it's going to stop, and his face turns serious. "Karyn, I'm so sorry for what I said to you earlier this week, but I want you to know I only said it because I was . . ."

"An idiot?" Karyn finishes, raising one eyebrow.

Reed laughs. "Yeah, an idiot." He swallows hard and forces himself to look her in the eye. "I was an idiot because I . . . I want to be with you."

She blinks, but her blue eyes are wide, ready, and willing. She's going to hear him out. Reed can't believe this is actually happening.

"I've wanted to be with you for so long, Karyn, I don't even know when it started. Kindergarten, maybe, I don't know."

She blushes and looks away for a moment, but she doesn't laugh. She doesn't tell him he's insane. She doesn't tell him she doesn't feel the same way.

"I know there are a million reasons for us to not be together," Reed says, taking a tentative step closer to her. "But for now, for one night, I'm going to pretend none of those reasons exist. I'm willing to do that because I need to know. I need to know if you feel . . . if you feel . . ."

He's run out of words. If he says anything more, he won't be able to take it back. Ever. He looks to Karyn for help. She has to give him a sign. If she glances away again, if she takes a step back, if she so much as says his name in a less than happy tone, he'll back off. This whole thing will end right here.

Reed holds his breath. Karyn looks up at him. And takes a step forward.

Pulse pounding a mile a minute, Reed watches as Karyn lifts her hands and lays them, right next to each other, on his chest. Just over his heart. She looks up into his eyes.

"I feel," she says quietly. Firmly.

Reed releases his breath with elated relief. He wraps his arms around Karyn and her hands slip up to encircle his neck. They smile at each other, and in that smile is years of friendship, years of confidence, years of memories and secrets and late night talks. Reed knows she's just as giddy and scared and psyched as he is.

He brings his lips down to meet hers, and her eyes flutter closed. It's the most tender, loving kiss Reed has ever experienced. He'd never known a kiss could feel this way.

*I love her,* Reed thinks. *I'm kissing the girl I love.*

*I'm kissing the girl my brother loves.*

But he won't let that thought take over. He won't let it bring him down.

As he and Karyn part, they both laugh, and the release is euphoric. He pulls her to him and hugs her tight, relishing the feel of her arms around him. At that moment, Reed decides to start living the life he deserves. Whatever the consequences may be, his life starts tonight.